A Barroom Bully

The one called Chinks declared in the jovial tone of the born bully, "My land, that's a pretty store-bought suit you have on, stranger! Where on earth did you ever come by a pretty suit like that?"

Longarm didn't answer.

Chinks said, "I was talking to you, stranger! What's the matter with you? Didn't your mother ever tell you it's rude not to answer when somebody talks to you?"

Longarm didn't turn around as he wearily replied, "Let's leave my mother out of this, and I won't ask what that *other* stranger told *your* mother what his name might have been."

So Chinks slapped leather.

Then he found himself on his ass in the sawdust with a fat, bloody lip, staring straight up the barrel of Longarm's .44-40.

"I'm going to say this just once. There are others in this cruel world with even faster draws and less forgiving dispositions. But I would rather the three of us agree not one thing happened in here this evening as we all go on about our own beeswax. Do we have us a deal, Chinks?"

TABOR EVANS

LONGARM

AND THE BOYS IN THE BACK ROOM

J

JOVE BOOKS, NEW YORK

THE BERKLEY PUBLISHING GROUP
Published by the Penguin Group
Penguin Group (USA) Inc.
375 Hudson Street, New York, New York 10014, USA
Penguin Group (Canada), 10 Alcorn Avenue, Toronto, Ontario M4V 3B2, Canada
(a division of Pearson Penguin Canada Inc.)
Penguin Books Ltd., 80 Strand, London WC2R 0RL, England
Penguin Group Ireland, 25 St. Stephen's Green, Dublin 2, Ireland (a division of Penguin Books Ltd.)
Penguin Group (Australia), 250 Camberwell Road, Camberwell, Victoria 3124, Australia
(a division of Pearson Australia Group Pty. Ltd.)
Penguin Books India Pvt. Ltd., 11 Community Centre, Panchsheel Park, New Delhi—110 017, India
Penguin Group (NZ), Cnr. Airborne and Rosedale Roads, Albany, Auckland 1310, New Zealand
(a division of Pearson New Zealand Ltd.)
Penguin Books (South Africa) (Pty.) Ltd., 24 Sturdee Avenue, Rosebank, Johannesburg 2196, South
Africa

Penguin Books Ltd., Registered Offices: 80 Strand, London WC2R 0RL, England

LONGARM AND THE BOYS IN THE BACK ROOM

A Jove Book / published by arrangement with the author

PRINTING HISTORY
Jove mass-market edition / December 2004

Copyright © 2004 by The Berkley Publishing Group

ISBN: 0-515-13859-2

JOVE®
Jove books are published by The Berkley Publishing Group,
a division of Penguin Group (USA) Inc.
375 Hudson Street, New York, New York 10014.
JOVE is a registered trademark of Penguin Group (USA) Inc.
The "J" design is a trademark belonging to Penguin Group (USA) Inc.

PRINTED IN THE UNITED STATES OF AMERICA

10 9 8 7 6 5 4 3 2 1

Chapter 1

Few passengers riding through on the U.P. Line ever noticed Sioux Siding was there. Most of the few who did wondered what it was doing there. The train crews knew it because they would stop to jerk engine water or, on very rare occasions, pick up a string of cattle cars from the siding there, which offered that part of the dinky settlement's name—Sioux Siding hadn't grown big enough to call a town as yet.

The Lakota or "Sioux" the siding was named for had never named the long swell in Wyoming's Sea of Grass anything. With neither water nor firewood handy, and exposed on all sides to the wayward winds out yonder, the high and dry stretch of the short-grass prairie exposed to an awesomely big sky just hadn't much mattered before the coming of the Iron Horse in '69. Even after the U.P. Right Of Way Survey had made note of a defendable stop, with well water within easy pumping range, the Indian scares that ended around '77 had discouraged others from moving in to take advantage of the year-around water and railroad stop. So when the herds were not in town, the population of Sioux Siding was small and tight, or just about the way most wanted it.

1

A handful of railroaders dwelled alongside the tracks to water engines and check for hot boxes, but neither the train crews nor the passengers were inclined to get off at Sioux Siding. So when a tall drink of water dressed more cowboy than railroad and wearing a six-gun as well, got off the afternoon eastbound out of Cheyenne, he attracted no more attention than an elephant running wild across the rolling sun-bleached prairie might have.

As the mysterious stranger stepped off the open pine platform like he knew where he was headed in the modest grove of mostly new construction, a gangling buck-toothed youth in a straw hat and Madras jacket fell in at his side and said, "Howdy! I'd be Bram Drew of the bi-weekly *Sioux Siding News and Advertiser*."

To which the stranger dryly replied, "Well, good on you. I ain't here to grant newspaper interviews."

"You must have come to town to do *something*," the would-be reporter insisted, adding, "I know most everybody in the county on tolerable terms, and I might be able to save you some trouble if you were to tell me just who you might be looking for here in Sioux Siding, Mr. . . . ah, I didn't get the name just now."

Without breaking stride the stranger said, "I didn't offer any names and allow me to suggest you save *yourself* some trouble by leaving me the hell alone."

He sounded serious as he added, "I hope I don't have to say that again."

Bram Drew had enough newspaper experience to know how far to push one's luck with strangers who walked and talked like that, so he shrugged, said he'd only meant to be friendly, and peeled off for the shade of the nearby Warbonnet Saloon as the mysterious stranger forged straight ahead as if he meant to walk straight up the middle of the north-south Market Street.

As the kid joined the dozen locals who'd been watching from behind the bat-wing doors and grimy front windows an older man with a gray walrus mustache and wearing an authoritative brass star, dryly commented on how short the *Advertiser*'s interview had seemed.

Bram Drew defensively replied, "You go on out after him and ask him all the questions you want, Uncle Roy. I have stared into the eyes of Mr. Death this day and lived to tell about it. So I desire a shot of White Lightning with a beer chaser as reward for the considerable chance I just now took in the interests of this community!"

"He's after somebody," decided Cherokee Adare, adding, "I told you when he got off he was after somebody. Men peddling windmills or searching for a long-lost true love in the middle of nowhere don't drop off no train in a gun-fighting crouch with their hat brim set so square and their six-gun tied so serious."

A more adventurous rider from the Rocking H stuck his head out the door to observe. "He may be new in town but he knows just where he's going. He's headed up Market Street like he owns it and . . . who could the law have papers on up thataways? Ain't nobody up that ways but—"

"He can't be the law," Uncle Roy cut in. "Lawman with a warrant don't barge into a town like he owns it. Lawman with a warrant on anybody in Sioux Siding would be looking for *me*, right now. It's neither polite nor at all wise to try for an arrest without the local law knowing what you're up to."

Cherokee Adare suggested, "Try her this way. Try a serious stranger with no warrant to serve. Try a personal call on some old friend, or enemy, he's tracked down to Sioux Siding!"

Bram Drew, having accepted and swallowed his shot of red-eye with a nod of thanks, wheezed, got his breath back with some suds, and demanded, "But who could we be talking about? I can't think of nobody here in Sioux Siding who'd have such a cold-eyed cuss tracking him."

Another older man snorted. "You have a heap of thinking to do, then, old son. Ain't none of the people here known one another more'n a year or so. Before any of us moved out this way there was this war that left many a man with a bitter heart and a whole new name and history."

He took a sip of his own suds and dryly added, "Oh, and did I fail to mention how many banks have been robbed, how much stock's been stolen or never rightly paid for back along the Goodnight Trail? I vote the moody cuss headed up Market Street is here to settle up with somebody who made him sore, somewhere, sometime!"

"So what are you going to do about it, Uncle Roy?" asked the younger and perhaps less realistic newspaper man.

Their town constable shrugged and said, "Don't see as I have to do shit before somebody does *something*. You just now said the stranger ain't a man who's easy to question about his own private beeswax. In the meantime the next train won't be stopping here this side of sundown. If that stranger has come to Sioux Siding to cause trouble there's no way he can leave for hours and that gives us plenty of time to show him the error of his ways if push comes to shove!"

Bram Drew grinned like a mean little kid as if he were already sticking front-page type. He chortled. "That's right! If he causes any trouble he has to get past you to board the next train out, right?"

The older lawman looked pained and asked, "Have you been reading Ned Buntline's Wild West Library again, Bram? Hark back to how the townsfolk of Northfield dealt with the James-Younger gang back in '76 and tell me one

4

more time how one stops an outlaw from leaving town once he's tipped his hand!"

Cherokee Adare said, "Hot damn! I'll fetch my ten-gauge Greener from my forge just up the tracks!"

Uncle Roy warned, "Let's not get our bowels in an uproar just yet. The day is young. The stranger might have come in peace. I don't want nobody waving guns about before I have me some justification!"

As if in answer to his very words, a distant shot rang out. Cherokee Adare said, "That sounded like a buffalo rifle to this child!"

"Your ears were not alone!" yelled Uncle Roy, drawing his old .36 Navy Conversion and tearing out the door with most, if not all, the boys in the Warbonnet trailing after him.

Since the gunfire had that effect on many a man, Main Street and Market Street were cluttered with milling and shouting men and boys as the town law tried to make some sense of the dusty confusion. He saw that quite a crowd seemed to be forming, a furlong up Market Street, in front of the Dexter Dry Goods. As he forged that way, he could see the crowd was gathered around something or somebody sprawled in the powdery blend of dry adobe and dung. As he got closer, he saw it was the mysterious stranger they'd been so worried about. He was no longer in any shape to worry anybody. The single, soft-nosed .50 caliber buffalo round that had hit him between the shoulder blades had blown out most of his breastbone and a whole lot of his shirt front. The resultant mess had settled in a bloody streak on up Market Street, as if to point the way the stranger had been headed when he'd been shot in the back.

His hat had settled upside-down between his wide-spread dusty boots. The piss had stopped pouring out of his dead bladder by now, but the lawman could see the stranger had been holding it in, as if too intent on more important matters than pausing along the way to piss.

At Uncle Roy's side, Cherokee Adare whistled softly and said, "Told you he was after somebody. They must have known ahead of time."

Bram Drew volunteered, "The killer knew where the stranger expected to meet up with him. So he was somewhere else when he threw down on his man from behind. But who could we be talking about, Uncle Roy? I can't think of any man in these parts I'd take for a back-shooting, cold-blooded killer!"

Uncle Roy sighed and said, "Back-shooting, cold-blooded killers don't last long when they advertise, Bram. We got us at least one in these parts in any case."

Designating a pair of part-time would-be deputies, the older lawman went on to say, "Since one doubts he means to come forward and confess, I want you boys to canvas back toward the tracks, with McBride on the east and Martinez to the west. Ask all along the way if anybody has a better notion where that Big Fifty was fired. Scout between the buildings for spent brass as well as any lingering smells of gun smoke. Big Fifty hurls it's three hundred grains of lead with seven hundred grains of powder from a bodacious amount of brass!"

He added morosely, "The killer will have carried the spent brass away with his sneaky ass if he has a lick of sense. But we could get lucky. How many masters of higher mathematics take it in their heads to shoot strangers in the back?"

As his deputies left along with other volunteers, Uncle Roy hunkered down to go gingerly through the dead man's blood-and-piss-soaked duds. A wallet in one hip pocket wasn't too soggy. Uncle Roy opened it to spy a German silver badge and the warrant and ID of a deputy U.S. marshal.

He marveled saying, "This poor dead fool couldn't have had a head for figures his ownself! What kind of blithering asshole gets off in a strange town to go after some wanted man without letting us local lawmen in on it? Had he won I could have shot him my ownself, as a suspicious stranger who had just put one of our own on the ground!"

Bram Drew said, "Like I told you back yonder, I had him down as trouble on the hoof, thanks to his bad manners! Why do you reckon he was acting so sinister and surly, Uncle Roy?"

The older man rose, dusting off his knee as he opined, "He most likely didn't mean to share no bounty money. He ain't packing any federal wants on him. Likely out to collect on a state Dead or Alive the simple way."

Cherokee Adare said, "Seems to me I heard somewhere how federal law ain't supposed to put in for cash rewards on the old boys they run in."

Uncle Roy grimaced and observed, "They ain't supposed to drink on duty or fuck willing Indian gals, neither. Didn't I just now tell you this dead cuss was out to work the case on his own?"

He saw that none of them seemed to follow his drift. He, explained, "His name was Pitcairn, and he was riding for the Denver District Court, officiously. Had the famous Marshal Billy Vail down Denver way sent him north across a state line on federal business I'd have been one of the first to know here in Sioux Siding. So try her this way. Try a Colorado-based and money-hungry lawman somehow learning somebody up our way was wanted not by Uncle Sam but say by some state, territory or railroad. Say his plan was to drift up our way on some made-up innocent errand, bump noses with a desperado wanted by some local authority he *didn't ride for* and, well, sort of had to do as an off-duty lawman has to do?"

Cherokee Adare chortled. "Works for me. Someone amid our friends and neighbors is wanted serious, somewheres, for a whole lot of money."

He nodded down at the dead man at their feet to add, "What old Pitcairn, here, failed to think through was that most wanted men *know* they're wanted and, once they've gone to ground in a little town where most everyone knows everyone else, they naturally keep an eye out for strangers!"

Bram Drew gasped. "I see it all, now! We weren't the only ones who saw a total stranger get off the eastbound with his gun tied down! So, knowing, or mayhaps just guessing, what Pitcairn had come here in hopes of doing, he met Pitcairn more than half-ways with more gun and so there Pitcairn lays, as dead as a turd in a milk bucket, and what do we do now, Uncle Roy?"

The local lawman shrugged and said, "Reckon it's my duty to wire the dead man's home office and tell them he just died up here. Marshal Vail will most likely arrange the coffin's rail connections down to Denver and, of course, he has to send some of his federal deputies up here to investigate the killing."

The young newspaper man eagerly interrupted, "Hot damn! Does that mean you and your boys will be working with them federal lawmen to catch the killer for Uncle Sam, Uncle Roy?"

To which the town law replied with a look of disdain, "Fuck Uncle Sam. If there was a federal bounty out on our neighbor who just shot a bounty hunter, Pitcairn wouldn't have been bounty hunting on the sly."

The young newspaper man looked confused and asked, "You don't aim to let a back-shooting, cold-blooded killer get away with it, do you, Uncle Roy?"

The town law didn't answer. He was aware how many of the townsfolk were listening. So it was Cherokee Adare

8

who took Drew aside to mutter, "You ask too many fool questions, for such a bright young feller."

The penny dropped. Drew asked in a whisper, "You mean Uncle Roy means to share the bounty with the boys in the back room and nobody else?"

Cherokee Adare didn't answer.

He didn't see as he had to.

Chapter 2

And so less than forty-eight hours later, another stranger got off the eastbound out of Cheyenne, and if this one was less mysterious, he was even taller and darker. He was saved from looking more Indian than old Cherokee Adare by his heroic mustache and wide-set gunmetal–gray eyes staring out from the shade of his telescoped black-coffee Stetson.

As per regulations of the current Hayes Reform Administration, the tall, tanned federal lawman wore a three-piece suit of tobacco tweed over his low-heeled cavalry stovepipes and hickory shirt. His double-action .44-40 by Colt Arms of Hartford rode grips forward, cross-draw, under the left-hand tails of his frock coat. The double derringer he packed in a vest pocket at one end of a gold watch chain was, like his own concealed badge, his own little secret until such times as either might be needed.

Since this stranger had been expected, Uncle Roy and a gaggle big enough to pass for a silent brass band were waiting on the platform as Deputy U.S. Marshal Custis Long of the Denver District Court joined them on the sun-silvered platform to introduce himself.

As they shook hands, Uncle Roy allowed, "I'd be Constable Sanderson. I have heard of you, Long. They call you Longarm and they say you're good. So how come it took you so long to get here?"

To which Longarm simply replied, "Homework. Saves running in circles like a recently decapitated chicken when you have some notion what you might be up to. Ed Pitcairn was one of our new boys. I never worked with him, and I suspect my boss, Marshal Vail, might have hired him more for his Scotch name than some of the references Pitcairn gave."

Uncle Roy frowned thoughtfully to ask, "What's wrong with Scotch names, Sanderson being one of them?"

Longarm answered easily, "Don't get your bowels in an uproar. Some of my best friends are Scotchmen. I only meant to imply they might not have known Ed Pitcairn as thoroughly as they thought. Where's the body at, by the way?"

Uncle Roy said, "Should have made it down to Denver by now. We shipped it packed in chipped ice and rock salt yesterday. What say we all get out of this hot sun, now? The Warbonnet, yonder, is closer as well as a tad more roomy than my dinky office up to the town lockup. Didn't you bring along no baggage?"

As they all ankled across the dusty Main Street toward the saloon, Longarm explained, "I travel faster, light, and most hotels ask a stranger to pay in advance whether he shows up with baggage or not. I find, out on a field mission, getting shaved by a local barber can be more informative than any fool shave I can manage from my own kit. I hope I won't be here so long I need to buy a fresh shirt. Any line on the killer, yet? You wired us you only had a little over two hundred grown men up this way to choose from."

As they all entered the Warbonnet and bellied up to

11

the bar, Uncle Roy let fly a weary sigh and said, "I forgot to include riders coming in or out of Sioux Siding all the time. What are we having, Longarm?"

The younger lawman said, "Draft beer will do me, on duty this early in the day. How many extra hands in this game might we be discussing?"

The local lawman sipped some suds in consideration before he decided, "Can't rightly offer firm numbers. Save for the handful of railroad men posted here to manage and defend the water tower and siding, the stockmen and their riders were out this way first."

As if the well-traveled Longarm were a greenhorn, the older lawman went on to explain, "The Union Pacific's original intent was no more than an engine water stop and a handy turn-off from their mostly single line of track as runs from Omaha to Ogden. You see, to run trains both ways on a single track you got to have places an east-bound or a westbound can get off the main line a spell—"

Longarm cut in, "I know how you run a railroad. Know how stockmen like to graze their herds near handy rail-road stops as well. So first a number of cattle outfits we're still working on moved into these parts. Then the usual general store, post office, saloons and such sprung up nat-ural and so we're talking about less than three hundred townsmen and . . . what?"

From the far side of Uncle Roy, Cherokee Adare vol-unteered, "I might be able to offer a guesstimate, Uncle Sam. I shoe riding stock, just down the way, and I average ten or twelve fresh shoeings a day, adding up to three or four hundred a month or let's say three or four hundred regular customers if a man knows what's best for his pony."

Longarm knew lots of high plains riders let their ponies wear the same shoes as long as eight weeks between re-placements but let it go as Adare continued, "Say your

12

average rider has a remuda of four to seven and, what the hell, let's say nigh a hundred out on the range using my services here in Sioux Siding."

There came a murmur of agreement from all sides. Longarm sipped more suds and asked if Adare was the only blacksmith in those parts.

Adare replied in a sullen tone. "There's two others. A dumb Swede and a fucking Jew. Neither one has been made to feel welcome here in the Warbonnet."

There came another murmur of agreement. Longarm didn't ask, but when he figured other blacksmiths would shoe roughly the same number he came up with about as many suspects in or out of town.

He thought back, nodded, and said, "Ed Pitcairn was shot in the back by a person or persons unknown on a Tuesday afternoon. Cowhands riding in to enjoy the bright lights of Sioux Siding would be more likely on Saturday night or their one day off a week."

Then he had to spoil it all for himself by morosely adding, "Unless, of course, we're talking about riders off nearby spreads. It's high summer and there's little call to pester a cow who's only gaining weight for you out on the open range. I reckon I'll canvas the closer cattle outfits after I finish up with everybody here in Sioux Siding."

"You aim to question *everybody*?" Bram Drew piped up, quickly adding, "If you let me tag along I might be some help, Deputy Long. I know everybody and they all know me and . . . well, you may have noticed folk here in Sioux Siding ain't used to talking to strangers."

Before Longarm could answer, Uncle Roy said, "Don't go making a pest of fool self, kid. Murder investigating is for grownups."

Turning back to Longarm the older lawman asked, "You were about to go into that so-called homework you done on our murder victim, weren't you?"

13

Longarm shrugged and said, "I hate digging through dusty files but now and again somebody has to. My boss said I was *it* when I confessed I knew what Ed Pitcairn looked like. Old Billy never sent him up this way for any reason. Pitcairn had asked permission to spend a week down in Santa Fe on his own personal beeswax. Seeing Pitcairn wasn't getting paid for the week off it never occurred to Billy to ask what said beeswax might have been."

Sipping more suds, Longarm dryly added, "Old Billy felt better after I'd pointed out a man who lied about where he was going might lie about why he wanted to go there. That's where the homework got dusty."

Uncle Roy nodded and said, "I'd have gone back over his job applications a second time if one of *my* deputies told me he was headed for New Mexico and wound up dead in Wyoming. What did you catch him on?"

To which Longarm could only reply, "Nothing. The little documentation Pitcairn had offered held up to wire checks Billy Vail was sore about as we parted down Denver way. Ed Pitcairn really served as a drummer boy with the Ohio Volunteers and rode for the Texas State Police during Reconstruction. Lost that job through no fault of his own when Washington allowed Texas to reconstitute it's own rangers. That's where we lose his paper trail a spell."

Uncle Roy asked, "How long a spell? Wasn't all that long ago the Texas Rangers opened for business again."

Longarm soberly replied, "Couldn't get Texas to give me exact discharge dates. One gets the impression that some files wound up as outhouse paper once the rangers moved back in. Pitcairn *said* he worked as a coal-mining company guard down Pueblo way after he left the Texas State Police. Since the company he said he worked for ran out of coal and went out of business, we got the better part of a year in sort of rough country for a man who wore tie-down to make friends or enemies unknown to ourselves. My boss thinks it's possible, and I agree, that Pitcairn headed up this way with a personal hard-on. It's more than possible, it only works one way, his killer suckered him with a personal invite."

Uncle Roy wasn't the only one there who seemed surprised as he replied, "He wasn't striding up Market Street like a man responding to a personal invite. Unless somebody sent him a graven challenge to a showdown!"

Longarm suggested, "Think back and study on what you just said, Roy. Would you move up the center of a strange street in a strange town in broad-ass daylight if you thought it at all possible somebody in the unfamiliar scenery ahead could be out to do you dirt?"

Bram Drew insisted, "He was seriously intent on meeting somebody up Market Street. With his gun tied down and—"

"His gun in the holster," Longarm cut in, adding, "Try her sensible and say somebody wrote to Pitcairn, telling him something or somebody he was interested in was up this way. Say he thought he was headed for a serious talk about serious shit, at a known address."

Uncle Roy said, "That sure could explain his walking up the center of Market Street so serious! Say he was looking for a street number when he didn't know which side of the street it might be on—"

Cherokee Adare chimed in, "The one who sent the invite has to be the one who killed him! Nobody else knew Pitcairn was about to get off that eastbound out of Cheyenne!"

Uncle Roy nodded soberly and said, "Knowing what time the train would arrive, the two-face who'd invited a man to his own murder had all the time he needed to set up his ambush. We never found no brass nor smelled us

15

no gun smoke because the sneaky son of a bitch likely fired from a window or a rooftop, set his rifle safely aside, and came down to join the crowd of innocent faces around his victim's remains!"

Shaking his gray head with a bemused smile, the older lawman added in a fatherly tone, "It happens that way, sometimes, old son. Unless he, she or it strikes again, the same way, we don't have a hope in hell at this late date. I hate it when they get away clean and leave no sign to cut!"

Longarm shrugged and set his empty stein on the bar as he quietly said, "Can't say how much sign there might be before I scout for some. But I may be up this way long enough to buy a fresh shirt after all. So what might the hotel situation be, here in Sioux Siding?"

The laughter all around seemed downright rude. But Uncle Roy was polite as he explained, "You and the late Ed Pitcairn were the only strangers to get off here within the past six months. What in blue thunder would anyone build a hotel in Sioux Siding for?"

Longarm smiled sheepishly and confessed, "Forgot I wasn't in Chicago where they send the cows. I'm going to need the hire of a horse as well. So I'll ask at the livery what they charge for the use of their hay loft. You do have at least one *livery* here, I hope?"

Uncle Roy nodded but said, "You'll be riding your pick from my remuda and my old woman will be proud to show off her cooking to a visitor from out of town!"

Longarm replied, "That's a mighty Christian offer, Uncle Roy, but let's hold the thought for now. It ain't that I don't admire home cooking, but I tend to come and go at all hours when I'm working a serious case and Billy Vail wants this one taken seriously."

The older lawman tried, "Well, shoot, we don't lock our back doors here in Sioux Siding, and you ain't about

16

to hire no ponies finer than the four I pasture out back. Our house is on the outskirts of town, which ain't but a couple of streets over, so we raise chickens and slop a hog out back as well."

"It ain't true their yard dog is a coyote. Not a *pure* coyote, least ways," someone commented from the crowd.

Longarm joined in the laughter but said he'd study on the offer. Young Bram Drew suggested, "What about Widow Epworth's place?"

Uncle Roy snapped, "That's a fool thing to say, even coming from you, Bram! Can't you see Longarm, here, is a white man who shaves regular?"

The young newspaper man fell into an abashed silence. So Longarm had to ask him what they were talking about. Cherokee Adare said, "Army widow of the Creek persuasion, followed her pale-face trooper up from old Fort Reno and he died on her over to Fort Sanders. These days she runs an open food stand near the municipal corral and sometimes takes riders overnight when they're too tired or too drunk to ride out across the open range. You don't want to stay there. Lord only knows when, if ever, she changes the bedding out back and, well, like I said, she's a *Creek*. Half Creek on her momma's side, least ways."

Uncle Roy confided, "The Creeks are the only tribe down to the Indian Nation in the habit of marrying up with black folk. Had a runaway slave they called the Black Warrior for a chief, back east, before Andy Jackson moved them west with the *civilized* tribes."

Longarm was too polite, seeing as Cherokee Adare admitted to being at least part Cherokee, to stick a pin in that balloon. Maroons, or runaway slaves, had joined forces with any Indian band who'd have them and, since Maroons knew more about the way the white cavalry carried on than most Indians had, most Indians had been glad to have them. The Comanche had played down Texas way

17

with a black bugler blowing some mighty confusing calls.

He settled for saying, "Mayhaps I'll try some this widow's cooking and ask her when she last changed the bedding. She might or might not cotton to the uncertain hours I keep."

Bram Drew said, "I'll be proud to carry you to Widow Epworth's and, being it's right by the municipal corral, with the Aurora Livery to her right and the Sunset Livery to her left, you'll have plenty of horseflesh to choose from if you decide to board with her!"

Longarm glanced at the Regulator Brand clock above the back bar to decide. "I'd like to meet up with the lady before quitting time makes it a busy time for talking."

Then he shook all around, told Uncle Roy he'd drop by later that night, or sooner, if he found anything worth reporting, and followed Bram Drew back out into the afternoon sunlight.

As they moved off, Uncle Roy muttered, "That damn fool kid had no call butting in like so! Couldn't he see I wanted Longarm bedded down close to my all-seeing eye?"

Chrokee Adare muttered, "I told him not to act so friendly with strangers but it seems tough to get through to the tail-wagging pup!"

He dropped his voice an octave as he added, almost to himself, "Some old boys are like that. It seems you have to put a bullet in their brains to gain their undivided attention!"

Chapter 3

The "homework" Longarm had mentioned had naturally included most every word recorded on paper about the ramshackle settlement they were passing through at the moment. But Longarm felt no call to point that out as his self-appointed tour guide ran off at the mouth about the wonders they were passing. An experienced lawman plays his cards close to his vest while he decides how close a witness might be sticking to the truth.

They were headed up Market Street, Bram said, because their Municipal Corral and the half-breed widow they were headed for were at the north end of Market Street where it turned to a narrower wagon trace across the sun-bleached rolling prairie.

They passed the front windows of the *Sioux Siding News and Advertiser*. As he waved to somebody on the far side of the grimy glass Bram Drew explained he alternated as a roving reporter and type sticker for his occasional paper.

As they approached the Dexter Dry Goods to their right the reporter said, "Yonder, near that pile of fresh horse shit, lies the scene of the crime. The dry blood was scattered by sundown last night. Nobody found any other sign between the buildings to either side of the street. Pitcairn must have been headed for somewhere farther along and . . . Son of a bitch, I just thought of something!"

Longarm had already thought of it, but he listened politely as the cub reporter eagerly went on, "What if we were wrong about him heading up Market Street as if he were searching for somebody along Market Street? What if a man with a mission, getting off the U.P. Line on foot, was out to hire himself a livery nag and ride on out of town?"

When Longarm didn't answer, the kid continued, "A man on his way to a meet-up or a showdown somewhere out on the open range would have had no reason to expect trouble here in Sioux Siding, before he could even mount up to ride . . . where?"

Longarm warned, "Slow down and back up, old son. If you aim to wind up a serious reporter you have to plant each card in your house of cards on cards already in place. You go sticking cards way in the middle of the air and you don't wind up with anything much!"

"What's wrong with my notion?" Bram Drew insisted.

Longarm said, "Nothing. It makes perfect sense a man getting off that train in Sioux Siding might have been headed farther on. Had Ed Pitcairn been back-shot in Cheyenne, before he had a chance to catch the eastbound out, we might be discussing where he'd been headed, east, west or on up to Montana. But we know he got as far, and *only* as far, as that pile of horse shit we just passed. So we eat the apple a bite at a time and work with the few facts we know for certain, for now."

They moved on, as the newspaper man who worked there told Longarm lots of things he already knew.

Washington had encouraged the building of western railroads with right generous land grants alongside their

20

granted rights-of-way. So the U.P. Line's original core of trackside construction had sprung up in the middle of a full 640-acre section. After that, as the land-granting had been expected to work out, the railroad had sold off town lots to settlers who'd seen the advantages of settling down close to a railroad stop instead of just claiming their own quarter sections, under the Homestead Act, somewheres a whole lot less profitable.

Bram Drew explained how stockmen farther out across the surrounding range had claimed individual quarter-section homespreads handy to firewood where possible and water no matter what, to range their slowly but surely growing herds all around on the short-grass. Neither Mr. Lo, the poor Indian, nor the buffalo herds he'd lived off of, were wandering back and forth worth mention these days.

The reporter allowed there were scattered puny herds of buffalo hither and yon, albeit not enough to encourage the serious market hunter these days. When Longarm observed he'd heard there were still some buffalo left up around the Milk River to their north, Bram Drew said he'd heard Sitting Bull's band was supposed to be sneaking south of the Canadian line to hunt some of the same and added, "I find the policies of our Bureau of Indian Affairs tough to follow at times."

Longarm dryly observed, "I've had Indians tell me the same. Seems every election means a new Indian policy, even if they don't get to vote. But the current Hayes Administration is one hell of an improvement over the previous Indian Ring. What's confusing the Indians in *these* parts?"

The kid answered, "They're the ones confusing me. I keep reading how Victorio is off the reservation with all those colored cavalrymen on his trail and yet, right here in Sioux Siding we got Cherokee Adare making money

21

hand over fist as a blacksmith, with that Indian army widow making out almost as well serving warm snacks and cold beer."

They strode on some before he added, "They're not the only Indians off any reservation, up this way. I don't get it."

Longarm said, "Neither does Victorio. The tenth cavalry ain't after him and his bronco Apache because they chose to depart from tribal lands set off to one side for them. The tenth cavalry is after them because they're acting so *bronco*! White boys who rape women and steal livestock are treated way worse than Mr. Lo, the poor Indian. The Army *wanted* to hang hundreds of Santee Sioux for rape, murder and worse when they put down that wartime uprising of Little Crow. But the psalm singers got to old Abe Lincoln and he up and pardoned all but a platoon of serious leaders. Mr. Lo gets off as ignorant of the law, which ignorant white or black boys plead to no avail when they pull the same shit."

"Then Victorio's crime wasn't jumping the Mescalero Reservation?" asked the cub reporter.

Longarm snorted. "Reservations are lands *reserved* for Indians and only Indians. They ain't prisons. There's no fences around them. Indians, or part Indians, such as Cherokee Adare and Widow Epworth up ahead, are off their own reservations for the same reasons orphans leave orphan asylums when they grow up. Anyone willing to work who speaks any English can make more money by accident, *off* a reservation, than he or she will ever manage *on* a reservation, on purpose."

The newspaper man said, "Oh, I figured folk like Cherokee and Widow Epworth got a break for being part white."

Longarm shook his head and said, "Quanah Parker was half white and as wild an Indian as the white man ever fought. Crazy Horse—they called him Tashunka Witko—in his daddy's lingo, had blue eyes and wavy brown hair to go with his war paint. Being Indian is as much a state of mind as a family tree. Down Denver way there's this pure-blood Arapaho family running this swamping bakery with white folk baking bread for 'em. President Grant up and promoted a full-blooded and damn smart Seneca Iroquois they called Donehogawa his commissioner of Indian Affairs. They'd met back before the war when Donehogawa was straw-bossing Indian ditch diggers along the Erie Canal. During the war Grant enlisted him as a U.S. Army engineer with the rank of lieutenant colonel and because of his neat penmanship Grant had this pure Indian write the surrender signed by Robert E. Lee."

Fishing out a three-for-a-nickel cheroot to light as they strode along, Longarm sighed and conceded, "The Indian Ring took advantage of Grant's Indian Affairs commissioner whilst they were taking advantage of Grant. But my point about a man with brains having his *choice* between behaving like a not-so-noble savage and a bakery owner still holds."

The reporter said, "I'd heard all the Colorado Arapaho had been frog-marched east to the Indian Territory with other hostiles."

To which Longarm replied, "I just said that. Let Cherokee Adare run bare ass down this very street, wearing feathers and paint, and they'll have him on his way to Fort Smith in no time at all."

By now they were within sight of the Municipal Corral, which took up one end of one of the last platted blocks near the north end of Market. The two barnlike liveries with corrals of their own out back tended to dwarf the two-story gray shingled structure between them. But as they got closer Longarm could see Widow Epworth's combined beanery and quarters might have passed for a fair-sized two-story *posada* wrapped around a patio.

Longarm was a natural man with human imagination so even though he tried not do do so, he tended to picture folk he'd heard tell about before he'd ever met them. He still recalled how pleasantly surprised he'd been when first he'd met the formidable sounding and clearly wronged wife of Silver Dollar Tabor, the no-longer-young but still handsome and downright bright Miss Augusta. Or what a letdown the dumb blonde Elizabeth "Baby" Doe old Tabor had left her for had seemed.

But try as he might, he found he'd formed an image in his mind of a part Indian Army widow running a beanery and part-time boardinghouse near the Municipal Corral. When Bram Drew introduced them and they shook hands across her oilcloth-covered counter, Longarm could see she was built like a well-known brick edifice with a face that belonged on the cover of *The Illustrated Police Gazette*.

Anyone could see how she'd photograph more French than Indian, once the camera flash had faded what looked like a serious suntan some. He could see some of her tawny coloring *was* a result of outdoor chores under the mostly cloudless Wyoming sky. It would have sounded dumb to confide he admired a woman who wasn't afraid to step out on her kitchen garden without donning a sun bonnet or packing a parasol. He could tell, despite her slim waistline, she felt no call to work so hard with a fool corset on and there was something about the way her naturally slender but sort of glandular body filled her thin calico bodice that could get a man stirred some inside his own duds. So although he never said it, Longarm knew this had to be the right place and got right down to business, filling Widow Epworth in on who he was, how long he figured to be in town, and what he needed in the way of a place to hang his hat.

Once they'd agreed that a dollar a day for room and board sounded fair to the both of them, Bram Drew allowed he had to go on back to his paper and stick some type. As he was leaving, Longarm started to ask him not to go into a whole lot of detail about this new address. But he never did. He knew there'd be no way he could vanish from human ken in a settlement so dinky, and he knew the sure way to make folks blab was to ask them not to. It seemed those most eager to conspire were most eager to tell everything they knew to everyone they knew.

But once they were alone Longarm did confide he liked to slip in and out as unobserved as possible. So the pretty young widow—her first name was Magnolia and he'd said it fit her—confided back that she'd soon have to serve a whole crew of unmarried local labor and suggested they get Longarm set up and out of the way whilst they still had the time.

She opened a drop-leaf gate at one end of her counter to lead him back through her long, skinny kitchen, across her stark, bare-dirt-paved patio and up an outside stairway to a wraparound second-story balcony. Then she led him to a corner room with cross ventilation by way of two small narrow windows, pointed at the empty washstand catty-corner from the Army cot and said she'd fetch him a wash bowl, a cake of soap and the water pitcher later.

He saw there was already a pillow with a fresh linen case, an upper and lower sheet, the top one cotton, with two summerweight flannel blankets folded atop the foot of the bed.

She offered him no room key, saying she'd never had call to lock up the room, adding, "The door barrel-bolts on the inside if you want to do something . . . private. I have to get on down and sling some hash, now."

Having nothing as yet that needed locking up, Longarm followed her out to reply, "I'd help you sling hash if

I wasn't up here on serious beeswax, Miss Magnolia, but while there's still some daylight to work with I got me some chores to do."

As they went down the stairs together he explained he meant to wire a progress report to his home office, adding, "Not that I have anything new to tell anybody, but my boss likes to know I'm trying."

She asked how long he meant to stay there in Sioux Siding, to which he could only reply, "I honestly don't know. It will depend on whether I cut sign or not. My boss wants the killer who gunned my fellow deputy. On the other hand he doesn't pay us to chase our own tails around in circles, and I fear the killer or killers got away clean. I just hate it when they do that but when they do there's not much we can do but toss in our chips and see if they have other chores for us."

At the foot of the stairs she turned to smile up at him and say, "I'm afraid I find that a tough one to swallow. Down home in the Indian Nation they tell a tale of a *wasichu washtey* called *Eestahanska* spending many days cutting the trail of a *wasichu shica* who had robbed the *Atey Tonka* and my mother's people with rations unfit for a *shunka*. Other lawmen had scouted the paper trails for signs and said there was none to be found. But you found some, didn't you, *Eestahanska?*"

So he knew that if she pronounced Longarm as *Eestahanska* in her mother's lingo she could hardly be a Creek and he said so.

She made a wry face and said, "You've been talking to Cherokee drunks, I see. I am Osage, on my mother's side. My father was a Cajun whiter than yourself. That breed blacksmith says bad things about me because I told him what I thought of any man, red or white, who can't hold *mini peta* as a man should."

Longarm avoided getting into that, and he excused

himself to head back to the trackside Western Union lay-out. It was still broad day but now the west side of Market Street lay in purple shadow and as he moved along that side he had the feeling he was being watched.

A heap.

He shrugged and told himself, "Natural feeling in a strange town when a man's on the prod for a killer." But as he strode on he caught himself humming the old trail song that went

> As I go walking down the street,
>> The people from their doorsteps mutter,
>>> There goes that Protestant son of a bitch,
>>>> The one who shagged The Riley's daughter!

And the feeling failed to fade by the time he'd made it to the Western Union. He ducked inside and glanced back outside and decided he'd only been feeling spooked because the long day was fixing to give way to the gathering dusk of a moonless night.

He was wrong. He had the keen instincts of a lone wolf, hampered by the common sense of an intelligent man and, in any case, the two men who'd been tailing him on the sunny side, fifty yards back, were well out of earshot as one hissed, "I *told* you he was headed for the fucking Western Union and Lord only knows what he's about to wire his pals about us!"

The older and wiser of the pair snorted. "He ain't got shit on us to wire anybody. He ain't even warm, so far, and like I told you, it would be dumb to put yet another lawman on the ground unless we have to!"

The more edgy one insisted, "What if we have to? What if he starts to get warm?"

His sidekick shrugged and said, "That's why we have

to keep an eye on the son of a bitch, to make sure he don't."

"And if he does?" the first one whimpered.

The other didn't answer.

The first one grinned, sort of dirty and said, "Oh!"

Chapter 4

The late Ezra Cornell hadn't died as famous as Sam Morse but he'd died a whole lot richer with his own pet college after forging Sam's notion into the mighty Western Union, and one of old Ezra's slickest notions had been the night letter, designed to keep all those Western Union wires humming around the clock.

Night Letters were telegrams sent way cheaper, when the telegraphers had no nickel-a-word regular messages to put on the wire. As the name was meant to indicate, they were mostly sent in the wee small hours to be delivered the next day instead of right now. So Marshal Billy Vail, as a natural born Scotchman, wanted agents in the field to wire in reports at night letter rates whenever possible and Longarm, having learned nothing all that exciting since his arrival in Sioux Siding, figured most any hour of a Friday would do the old fuss.

While he was block lettering his field report, Longarm included some of his second thoughts on the paperwork he'd done before leaving for Wyoming. Having noticed how lacking they seemed in sinister strangers up their way, Longarm suggested some mighty tedious homework indeed. He knew poor Henry, the priss who played their typewriter and managed their files, was going to say mean things about his mother, but Longarm couldn't think of a better way than cross-checking the local county directory with such records as the War Department might have on that Ohio Volunteer outfit the late Ed Pitcairn had served with.

A heap of the wildness Ned Buntline bragged about in his magazines had been the result of bitter war memories and the less formal law enforcement of a less populated and more rustic West. Some held it was worth serious consideration that the late Sheriff William Brady of Lincoln County, New Mexico, had been a first sergeant in the Union Army. For whilst it seemed true Billy the Kid had never served in any army, Billy the Kid kept telling anyone who'd listen he wasn't the one who'd back-shot Bill Brady.

According to his own job application, Ed Pitcairn would have been sixteen or not full grown as yet, when they'd mustered him out of that irregular Ohio infantry. Longarm assured poor Henry, by way of their mutual boss, he wouldn't have to dredge for the names of every survivor of the regiment. An older soldier bullying a skinny young drummer boy would have been in the same company, narrowing things down considerably and, after that, the only names that mattered should appear on both the army and recent county rolls. For it hardly mattered if anybody had cornholed a young drummer boy with a long memory if they'd never wound up around Sioux Siding.

Ed Pitcairn would have been back-shot by an old Army grudge in Sioux City, Iowa, if he'd located the rascal there instead.

Before he'd finished his night letter, Longarm knew the notion of revenge for some war injury might be grasping for straws. But when you had nothing better to grasp for, you grasped at what might be there and Longarm knew of many a veteran's gathering that, had turned out tragic once strong drink got to mixing with strong memories. Longarm knew, himself, how the slights and insults suffered in one's formative years could itch like hell, long after the everyday bumps and bruises a grown man suffered had been written off as not worth stewing over.

After comparing sheepish notes with others around many a campfire, he knew how a man who'd already forgotten that prick-tease he'd wasted his money on a cattle drive long ago could still find himself going over that awful night during school vacation when the only gal he'd ever want had flared up at some dumb thing he'd said and told him they were through.

That bigger kid who'd demanded your best shooting marble or made you suck his pecker in the wood shed, would never in this world get off your list of those you'd slowly torture to death, if ever you got to rule the world. Even though you'd long since laughed off that false friend who'd stolen your first wife and forgiven many a bad debt. So considering revenge, as a motive, pro or con, could be mighty tricky.

But when you were trying to come up with a motive you had to consider everything that might work, and they'd established before Longarm had left Denver that Ed Pitcairn could not have headed up this way after any bounty posted next to any name on the county register.

Leaving the telegraph office in the tricky light of a pending prairie sundown, Longarm lit another cheroot and told the waterproof Mex match as he shook it out, "I can't see how a green lawman in Denver could detect a false name on a homestead claim, business license or such. There's no way he could have recognized a face in such a distant crowd. So we could be right about an old army grudge not covered by the law, or somebody up this way could have gotten in touch with him and . . . then what?"

As he strode on to the Warbonnet Saloon Longarm remembered the trouble he'd already had, establishing Western Union had never delivered a wire from anywhere to Ed Pitcairn's last Denver address. Marshal Vail in the flesh had had to pull some wires to establish Pitcairn had never picked up any wires from Wyoming at any Western Union office, anywhere.

That only left the U.S. Mails, and they'd told him at the post office not to be silly. Their mailmen were expected to drop envelopes from their bags at addresses indicated, not to memorize or even give a toad turd where a particular letter might have hailed *from*. One of the mailmen covering the route of Pitcairn's rooming house had recalled the name, Pitcairn. That was more than the other one could say.

Shoving all the stew pots on the back burner to simmer a spell, Longarm went into the saloon to find the place right empty as he bellied up to the bar and rewarded himself for an afternoon of tedious legwork with a shot of Maryland Rye and a schooner of draft to help him breathe some more.

The portly, balding barkeep explained, as he wiped the nearby zinc top, how most of the regulars were home for supper at that hour. Longarm was too polite to ask where the barkeep thought the robin birds went in the wintertime. He knew most of the local establishment accepted as regular gents instead of jerk-offs or queers would be married up or shacked up, and he'd already established the transients and working stiffs with no roofs of their own to eat under would be supping at such beaneries as his handsome new landlady ran. He'd chosen to spend the supper hour at the discreetly distant Warbonnet to avoid being anywhere near Magnolia while she slung hash to her regular admirers.

Since she wasn't slinging hash at Longarm, and he was already having second thoughts about rye whisky on an empty stomach, he asked how come they didn't seem to have a free lunch spread at the Warbonnet Saloon.

The barkeep replied, "We tried that a spell back. The boiled eggs and pickled pigs' feet seemed more tempting to the flies. Most of our regulars are served regular meals at nearby homes and come here to drink serious or socialize. They've all known one another a spell and just need a place to share gossip or do business sort of private. We don't try to run a fancier set-up than the boys in the back room require."

That seemed for damned sure, Longarm decided as he idly ran his eyes over the utilitarian interior. Cow-town saloons weren't nearly as colorful as they were illustrated in some magazines. They had that human skull over the back bar in Bodie, and a tedious number of lithographs of that same old naked maja gal offered decor to many a western saloon, but most were as Spartan as the famous Long Branch in Dodge, which could have passed for the inside of a big shoe box if they'd taken the bar and tables out. The Long Branch hadn't been named for a longer than average bar. The owner, Luke Short, hailed from Long Branch, New Jersey.

The Warbonnet up in Sioux Siding was about the same size, say twenty feet wide by thirty feet deep with a private back room behind a door marked PRIVATE. Only one of the small round tables spread across the sawdust-covered floor was occupied at the moment. Two men who were obviously cowhands seemed to be sharing sandwiches and a scuttle of beer. When Longarm asked how one managed to wrangle a sandwich in these parts the barkeep confessed, "I can make you one in the back for two bits. We're out of white bread but the whole wheat's only a day old and you have the choice of ham or roast beef on Swiss or rat trap cheese. I hope you ain't one of them religious nuts who fancy rabbit greens or other vegetation in a sandwich."

Longarm agreed lettuce was for rabbits and allowed he'd settle for both kinds of meat and both kinds of cheese.

When the barkeep pointed out it would take more than two slices of bread to contain such an order, Longarm nodded soberly and replied, "I just said that. Let's settle on four sandwiches for six bits and I might tip you a quarter if all four are edible."

The barkeep laughed, topped Longarm's schooner off with fresh suds from the tap, and went in the back to put his simple supper together.

Longarm half turned to lounge against the bar, facing the bat-wing doors leading out to the street. That was where trouble usually appeared first, in a strange saloon in a strange town. Things outside were commencing to look orange and purple as the sun sank ever lower in the west. Inside the saloon it was still light enough to read a newspaper, if you strained some, but Longarm knew places in town that meant to stay open a spell would have to consider lamplight before long.

He didn't turn his head as he heard chair legs scraping away from the one table. It was a free country and whether those young cowhands meant to take a leak out back or head on home was none of his beeswax.

He had no call to listen in on private conversation until one of them could be heard to say, "Aw come on, Chinks, the stranger ain't done nothing to you."

To which a less sober voice could be heard to reply, "He done something to men when he got hisself born. I don't *like* strangers! Never have and I never will!"

So, seeing he was the only stranger in those parts, Longarm turned to stare into the mirror over the back bar and, sure enough, both of them seemed to be looking at him.

It was easy to see which one was called Chinks. It wasn't as easy to see why any rider would be wearing black knee-length chaps in high summer on the high plains of Wyoming.

Summerweight chaps were worn in chaparral country to protect a rider's legs from the stickerbrush they were named after. Winter chaps of sheep or goat skins with the hair left on were to keep one's legs warm out on the open range with the wolf wind blowing. Chaps of any description were just for show at that time and place. So the hand called Chinks was a show-off and looked it, with that bodacious black ten-gallon, black sateen shirt and wide humorless grin.

The brace of double-action Colt lightning he was toting in a low-slung buscadero rig of black tooled leather called for more serious consideration. But Longarm just sipped some suds, with his gun hand free for whatever might happen next as Chinks came to a halt, too close for comfort, shrugged off the friendly hand his pard tried to urge him on out with, and declared in the jovial tone of the born bully, "My land that's a pretty store-bought suit you have on, stranger! Where on earth did you ever come by a pretty suit like that? I'll bet it was made by a Jew, in Paris, France!"

Longarm didn't answer.

Chinks said, "I was talking to you, stranger! What's the matter with you? Cat got your tongue? Didn't your mother ever tell you it's rude not to answer when somebody talks to you?"

Longarm didn't turn around as he wearily replied, "Let's leave my mother out of this, and I won't ask what

35

that *other* stranger, passing through, told *your* mother what his name might have been."

So Chinks slapped leather.

Then Chinks found himself on his ass in the sawdust with a fat, bloody lip, staring straight up the barrel of Longarm's .44-40 as his pal pleaded, "Please don't shoot him, mister! He's just a fool kid who can't behave his fool self after a few beers!"

Longarm said, "I noticed. That's how come he's still alive. I am going to say this just this once, for both your ears. Do I have both your ears?"

When they both nodded eagerly, Longarm continued, "There are others in this cruel world with even faster draws and less forgiving dispositions. But fortunately for present company I ain't out to add to my luster with an easy win over a rude child. I would rather the three of us agree not one thing happened in here this evening as we all go on about our own beeswax. Do we have us a deal, Chinks?"

The suddenly more sober kid at his feet gulped, nodded, and allowed he had meant no disrespect to his elders.

So Longarm nodded and said, "Bueno. Put your hat back on and leave both of them six-guns alone on your way out. I would offer to buy you boys a drink but I can see you've had enough and have to be on your way, right?"

His pal helped Chinks to his feet. As he did so the barkeep came out from the back with the sandwiches, took one look at the fat lip, cursed like a mule skinner and said, "God damn it, Chinks Potter! If I've told you once I've told you a hundred times not to roughhouse in here. How come you hit him this time, Bunny?"

The one called Bunny gasped. "It wasn't me, Mahoney! I tried to get him to leave this stranger the hell alone!"

"The fool kid started up with *you*, and he's still alive?" marveled Mahoney as he set the tray of sandwiches on the bar near Longarm.

Longarm tried to smooth it over with a hearty, "Never amounted to any start up. Chinks, here, just tripped over my big old foot and I was just telling him I was sorry. So it's over. Ain't that right, boys?"

It didn't work, and the barkeep wagged a finger at Chinks to warn, "I've told you your rawhide manners will be the death of you, Chinks Potter, and when you get on out to your bunkhouse at the Rocking H you had better get down on both knees and praise the Lord for showing so much mercy to drunks and reckless riders. For you just now lived through a brush with the real deal, and I'm surprised we don't need to spread any more sawdust across that very floor this evening!"

Longarm tried to catch the barkeep's eye as he softly said, "Let it go, Mahoney. I said it was over. I *want* it to be over!"

The barkeep looked more puzzled than understanding as Bunny led Chinks to the doorway by one arm. It might have worked, had Chinks not turned to demand, "What do you mean by the real deal, Mahoney? Do you know who this sucker-punching stranger might be?"

Longarm wanted to punch all three of them as the barkeep chortled sort of proud and said, "I surely do. I just now built them sandwiches for the one and original Longarm, the fastest gun in the West, now that Wild Bill lies dead and buried!"

Longarm muttered, "Aw, mush!" as Chinks Potter stared flabberghasted, dabbed at his split lip, and gushed, "Great day in the morning! Can't wait to tell all the boys in the bunkhouse out yonder I just slapped leather with the fastest gun in the West and lived to brag about it!"

37

As they left, Longarm turned, picked up a sandwich, and growled. "This had better be good. You just made sure that everybody for miles around is going to know I'm in town, comes the cold gray dawn."

Chapter 5

It turned out that Longarm didn't have to wait until the cold gray dawn. He'd just finished his last sandwich and the sun was still setting outside when the town law, Roy Sanderson, better known as Uncle Roy, roared in to demand, "What this I hear about a showdown in this joint, Mahoney?"

By that time Longarm had managed to talk to the barkeep some and so Mahoney replied, "Wasn't that big a deal, Uncle Roy. Young Chinks Potter off the Rocking H made the mistake of commenting on the duds of this here lawman. We sent him on his way older and wiser with no harm done."

Uncle Roy said, "I heard they carried him home bleeding bad." Then he turned to Longarm to demand, "As one lawman to another, what happened?"

Longarm shrugged and asked, "Have you ever noticed how you can bust a jar of olives on the boardwalk on one end of a city block and have the story turn into a wagonload of watermelons hit by a train by the time it gets to the other? Like Mahoney just said, a fool kid with a fresh mouth made some foolish remarks. I only backhanded him some. His lip was only split a tad and was hardly bleeding worth mention as they left."

Uncle Roy thought that over, sighed, and asked how close Longarm felt he might be to solving the assassination of Deputy Pitcairn.

Longarm sighed back and said, "I've barely started. Haven't found a lick of a sign. Had a notion I wired my home office to look into. Take 'em a day or so to find out whether I wired smart or full of shit."

Uncle Roy sounded as if he meant it when he said, "Tomorrow being a Friday and the riders on the Rocking H working 'til Saturday noon, I can let you have the better part of thirty hours to fish or cut bait. If you ain't hot on the trail by the time the one-fifteen westbound stops for a drink here, come Saturday, I want you aboard her as she leaves. For by Saturday afternoon, the riders of the Rocking H figure to be hot on your trail!"

Longarm snorted. "Bullshit! Neither Chinks Potter nor his outfit have any just feud with this child!"

To which the local lawman replied, "Who says it needs to be *just*? We've had trouble with the Rocking H since the Irish spitfire who owns it moved her herd up to greener grass from Texas. Half her riders are teenaged Texican rebels and the ones who ain't are convincing imitations, with every mother's son of them aided and abetted by the stubborn crazy-lady they all ride for."

Mahoney added, "Miss Maureen ain't crazy because she's Irish, Uncle Roy. They say she went crazy when Comanches tortured her true love to death. They say she rode with the posse that found him at the bottom of a rise with his cock and balls cut off and stuck in his dead mouth."

Uncle Roy said, "I hate it when Indians act worked up like that. More to the point, the State of Texas stipulated, in exchange for dropping the charges, Miss Maureen Flan-

40

nery was to leave the Comanche Nation the hell alone and get out of Texas forever. I'd better have me a bourbon and beer steady my nerves, Mahoney."

As the barkeep poured, Uncle Roy conceded, "It ain't as if Miss Maureen ain't a proper lady as far as paying her just debts and avoiding scandal or even mean-mouthing other ladies goes. Her problem seems to be that, having more than once killed Comanche men, women and children, personally, Miss Maureen can't seem to take her cowhands shooting out a street lamp or roping and dragging an outhouse seriously."

He downed the shot glass of bourbon Mahoney had just slid across the zinc bar to him and added without chasing it, "She's bailed hands out for drunk and disorderly more times than you could shake a stick out, and got Chinks off on assault with a deadly just this spring."

As he sipped his own suds, Longarm asked who Chinks might have assaulted.

Uncle Roy said, "Hardware salesman. Up by the Dexter Dry Goods. Forgot his name. Chinks laughed at his yeller shoes and invited him to dance. So when the out-of-towner had too much sand in his craw to dance he wound up with a little toe shot off. They say Miss Maureen paid him many a month's wages to drop the charges. I agreed to write it off as an accident and sort of forget the town ordinances about gunfire along Market Street after old Chinks promised me he'd mend his ways."

Holding up a finger, Uncle Roy told Mahoney, "Make that another bourbon."

Then he turned back to Longarm to add, "You can see the bind this puts me in, Longarm. I only got a handful of part-time deputy constables to back my play when, not *if*, Chinks Potter rides in late Saturday with at least a dozen like-minded wild-ass riders backing *his* play."

Longarm quietly objected, "It seemed to me we were parting friendly."

Uncle Roy said, "Chinks Potter's like that when the odds ain't in his considerable favor. He knows he has the edge on most everybody in these parts, thanks to riding for a crazy lady who admires and encourages her kids to express themselves. But mark my words, give Chinks Potter a day or more to consider his options and recruit some help out to the Rocking H and, well, you'll be on that train to Cheyenne and we'll say no more."

Longarm went silently to work on his own suds. He'd been raised on the Good Book and some of its advice made sense. The Good Book advised you to take one day's troubles at a time and added that soft answers turneth away wrath. So there was no sense getting anyone's shit hot before say late Friday or early Saturday.

When a tall drink of water in bib overalls and a derby hat came in to join them at the bar, Uncle Roy said, "Well?"

His part-time deputy replied, "I tailed them Rocking H riders like you said. They stopped for some black coffee at Widow Epworth's, got their ponies out of the Aurora Livery, and rode north until I couldn't make them out no more in the gloaming."

Uncle Roy thought and sighed, "Let's hope I'm right about it taking Chinks until knock-off time to stir things up out yonder."

Turning back to Longarm he asked, "What say we split the difference? You cut serious sign by this time tomorrow night and we'll be proud to posse up with you. In return I want your word you'll catch the Friday night train west and save us a whole lot of trouble if you're still in the dark!"

Longarm said, "I got a man's word, in front of two

witnesses, and it's for my boss, not me, not you, to say when I'm done here."

Uncle Roy insisted, "You're good. You ain't that good. In the unlikely event you kill off all her riders, Miss Maureen is likely to avenge the whole bunch personally in all her towering rage and a scalping knife and *then* what are you going to do?"

Longarm smiled crookedly and replied, "Ask her if she fancies the two-step or the waltz," and set his empty schooner aside to stride out into the gathering dusk.

He circled to make sure nobody from the saloon was following him. So he missed the rider in black lurking across the way in the slot between a hat shop and a feed store. He knew his pals in Denver could use all the help they could get if he wound up dead as Ed Pitcairn up this way. So he went back to the Western Union and had the night clerk send another night letter describing his fix and asking them to check out any Maureen Flannery being let off on a mass murder charge by the State of Texas. As a rule it was the Bureau of Indian Affairs in conjunction with the War Department you had to deal with when you hunted Indians out of season.

As he left the telegraph office for the second time the stars were out it was the dark of the moon, and somebody had shot out the street lamps the length of the block.

Longarm didn't care. He knew where he was headed and he could see the lamp-lit far end of a sort of shadow tunnel as he headed on into it.

Once he had, as he'd expected, he could see the walk beneath him and the shut-down shops to either side more clearly, thanks to the little light at each end of the tunnel. He glanced up to see if he could see the stars better from a blacked-out stretch of street. He could. The Wyoming sky looked downright country, with one end of Orion's

Belt winking down through the glass of a shot-out street lamp.

The unbroken glass of a shot-out street lamp?

Longarm took three more paces before he decided to go with the hairs atingle on the back of his neck and side-stepped into a narrow inky slot between two buildings.

As he did so a not-too-distant rifle roared and something buzzing like a pissed-off yellow jacket whipped through the space he'd just been walking through!

It hadn't been a yellow jacket. It had been at least five hundred grains of hot lead! So Longarm crawfished forty-odd feet into somebody's back yard where a man could do some serious dodging as he got his own gun out, feeling way out-gunned in spite of his .44-40 being a more powerful handgun than most.

He made it to a back alley as doors and windows commenced to open all around and more than once voice bitched about fool kids setting off cherry bombs with the Fourth of July over and damnit done with.

Hunkered with his back protected by a high board fence, Longarm took his own good time, knowing he was safe, for now, as he considered his options.

He didn't have many options that made much sense. He was still working on how you turned off a block of street lamps while your target was off the street sending wires. They were no doubt still trying to figure why he'd jinked sideways off the walk as they fired down the length of it to knock him down like a bowling pin. By now the street out front would be cluttered with more sincerely confused innocents than guilty parties. Nobody with a lick of sense would be standing there with a Big Fifty, as if to holler, "Me! It was me!"

Worse yet, Uncle Roy and other local law would be homing in on the sound of gunfire and Longarm didn't want to argue about whether he stayed in Sioux Siding or not. So he eased on up the alley until he found another slot, made his way over to a side street going in his general direction, and went pussy-footing north by zigs and zags, hugging the darker shadows until he made it back to Magnolia Epworth's place.

Her beanery faced the street and was shuttered for the night. Longarm went around to the back, slipped through the archway into her courtyard, and then he moved up the outside stairs on the balls of his feet, gun drawn.

He hadn't told anybody he could think of that he'd be bedding down at this address. On the other hand he couldn't tell how many customers Magnolia might have bragged to. When Indians or part-Indians admired a man, they would go on about how brave they were and what good medicine they had.

It wasn't anywhere near his usual bedtime. He wasn't certain he was in for the night. But wandering dark streets aimlessly, when somebody you didn't know was gunning for you, could take years off your fool life!

So he figured he'd fort up a spell while he studied on his next moves. He was looking forward to some quiet time sitting down when he spied the light leaking out the bottom of the door he'd hired for the night.

It wasn't a whole lot of light. It figured to be coming from a candle on the far side. Someone with a candlestick was in there, pussy-footing where he'd left nothing for them to go through, or waiting up for him!

Magnolia Epworth had said the door was left unlocked when the room lay empty and barrel bolted when it was occupied. Knowing anybody inside would know as much, Longarm considered how dumb it would be to barrel bolt against a man you were out to ambush and simply barged in, fast and low, to crab to one side with his back to the pine paneling as he threw down on the figure seated on the Army cot.

She let out a considerable gasp before Longarm could say, "I'm sorry, Miss Magnolia. Thought you might be somebody else."

The beautiful breed half sobbed. "I've been so worried about you, *Eestahanska*! First those riders off the Rocking H were talking about you when they stopped for coffee downstairs! Then, just minutes ago, Bram Drew from that newspaper was by, asking if I'd seen you and whether you were boarding here or not! He said there had been a shooting down by the telegraph office. He thought you might have been mixed up in it!"

Longarm said, "I was. That's why I took my time getting here by way of some zigs and zags in the dark. What did you tell the newspaper man?"

She said, "Nothing. I am only half *Wasichu*. Who did you fight with near the telegraph office, *Eestahanska*? Chinks Potter had ridden out of town long before I heard that distant rifle shot at this end of Market Street."

He said, "That's a good question. It was an ambush. They winked out all the street lamps for a business block, and I'm still trying to figure out how the hairs on the back of my neck figured that out just in time."

He went on to offer a terse account of those tense ten minutes or so down by the tracks and added, "You've been here longer than me. Might you know just how they light up Market Street after dark, Miss Magnolia?"

She said, "Of course. Old Peg Leg Ferris starts up this way, just at sunset, with his lamp lighter, an oil-fired wick on a long pike with this hook he opens and closes the street lamps with from the walk."

She thought and added, "As a matter of fact I served him coffee and a donut around six this evening. You say he only failed to light the lamps along that one stretch?"

Longarm grimaced and replied, "More likely somebody else has a long pole of their own to go with that buffalo rifle."

She said she was sorry she couldn't be more help.

He replied, "Don't talk *tachesli*. You're about all the help I've been offered since I got here and I suspect I may be on to something the ones with that long rifle and even longer lamp lighter hope I ain't. I suspect they're operating out of some indoor base near the tracks. How far could even a local boy wander with a buffalo rifle or ten-foot pole without a single witness noticing?"

She told him how smart he was. She hadn't made a move to rise from that one narrow cot. He glanced at the open door with a meaningful look before he told her, "You did right in telling Bram Drew I wasn't here. But if I can make educated guesses, others can make educated guesses and I'd best just shut and barrel bolt that door for now. So if you were fixing to leave, Miss Magnolia . . ."

She demanded in a determined tone, "Why should I want to leave? Don't you want to have *tawitan kola* with me, *Eestahanska*?"

"My friends call me Custis," Longarm replied as he turned to shut and bar the door to holster his six-gun and, while he was at it, unbuckle the whole rig. As he turned around, he saw Magnolia had already shucked her simple calico shift to await his pleasure in all her tawny naked glory.

When she rattled something that sounded adoring in Osage he smiled down at her to warn, "Slow down and say that some more in *Wasichun*, ma'am. I fear I got some catching up to do with Osage customs."

She answered, "I was asking if we wanted this candle out . . . Custis."

To which he could only reply, seeing how swell the soft candlelight outlined her bodacious hills and dales, "Leave it be. I'd like to see just what I was getting into, for a change."

Chapter 6

Longarm worried some about that narrow army cot as he shucked his own duds and hung his gun belt handy. But despite her French form and features, Magnolia had been raised Osage and so, like most Indian gals, she liked to be the one on top and in this case it was a sight to see, with her bare heels hooked on the hickory frame to either side of Longarm's bare hips while she braced her palms against his bare chest to gyrate in every direction, including up and down, considerably, as she swallowed him whole and spit him almost out with her love slicked ring-dang-doo.

She bragged on having been married up with the U.S. cavalry and as Magnolia showed him how she could ride, Longarm couldn't help wondering whether other Indians had killed her soldier blue or whether she'd done it all by herself.

He was too polite to ask, of course. So he never found out and it never really mattered just how she'd wound up a young and beautiful, but damned experienced, widow. It wouldn't have been polite to ask whether her late husband or Cajun kith and kin had advised her it was only right to finish a man off with a French lesson when you came ahead of him.

She'd come ahead of him, she confessed, because she hadn't been getting any for some time. He doubted she wanted to hear about that other gal down Denver way sending him off to Wyoming so tenderly.

Taking some time to get their second winds, the two of them snuggled with her half-atop him again as they shared a smoke with her head nestled on his bare shoulder and her shiny black hair all over his chest. As she idly toyed with his limp organ grinder Longarm had her bring him up to date on the way things worked around Sioux Siding.

Like most lay residents of most communities large or small, Magnolia Epworth took such civic services as there were for granted. She'd told him about that old lamp lighter, for example, without ever asking herself who might have hired Peg Leg Ferris or how much they paid him. She knew a colored man with a buckboard hauled her kitchen leftovers and garbage off to a hog farm downwind of the U.P. siding and loading chutes. She'd never asked if he was working for the powers that might be or helping himself and his hogs to free slop from all the beaneries in town.

She said a rider from the county sheriff came by once a year to collect firm but fair property taxes. She couldn't say who paid Uncle Roy or any of the other mostly older white men who seemed to be in such charge as a given situation called for.

Longarm passed the smoke back to her as he mused, half to himself, "We established down Denver way before I left that Sioux Siding was as yet an unincorporated mushroom around a trackside core the U.P. Line runs as a company town. Or a company branch, least ways. Rail siding, half a dozen cattle pens and loading ramps, along with a pump house, water tower and a trackside string of toolsheds and workers' quarters hardly qualify as a town."

She snuggled closer, gave his virile member a friendly squeeze, and said, "Now that you have me thinking about it, Custis, I'm reminded of Fort Reno and other army posts out our way that my man and me passed on through. They were all set up much the same. Can I set this cheroot to one side, now? I can't talk, smoke and pet at the same time."

Longarm took the cheroot back, had a last deep drag, and snuffed it out on the floor, within easy reach from the army cot, as Magnolia went on, "Most every army post, like most every Indian agency, is set up the same neatly squared off way, with a sort of tipi and pig-pen zone around it, occupied by the sort of folk—red, white or black—usually drawn to an army post or Indian agency."

Longarm replied, "That's about the size of it. Railroad stops attract somewhat more solid citizens. But until there's enough to petition the state or territorial government for incorporation forms, things just sort of get decided by the boys in the back room. They likely pass the hat for such regular services as those of Peg Leg Ferris or Uncle Roy."

"So who's lawfully running our local government?" the stark naked, but suddenly curious, local business-woman asked.

It was a good question.

Longarm said, "I'd best see if I can find out, come morning. Running things informal is by definition a less than tidy way to run anything. I have seen 'em pass the hat, set aside a share of the winnings in the back room or all too often, not ask questions as the bigger frogs in the pond seem to manage without constitutional questions about city charters, voter registrations and such."

"Is that legal?" Magnolia asked.

Longarm replied, "Up to when and where somebody decides it ain't fair and petitions for redress."

"Redress?" she asked.

He kissed the part of her hair and replied, "That's what you ask for when you think you ain't getting a fair shake, redress. But the courts just ain't got time to go *looking* for folk who don't find things fair."

She allowed that didn't sound fair. Seeing there were so many *heyoka shica* out to take advantage of everybody.

He explained, "Neither us lawmen nor the courts we ride for have time to consider every kid being whupped unfair by stern parents and just where you draw the line between a family, a gathering, a campsite or a settlement is a fuzzy consideration. The boss of a camp or a company town has the right within reason to run things his own way. Many a mining camp has run itself, sometimes with the help of its own self-appointed vigilance committee, past the point where the strike bottomed out and they never needed no papers of incorporation. Many a New England mill town is way bigger than Sioux Siding and nobody but the mill owners worries about who picks up any garbage."

"Then when and how come most towns wind up with municipal governments running things constitutionally?" she asked, too interested to massage his manhood at the moment.

He put his free hand on her tawny wrist to move her soft hand the way he liked it as he replied, "I already told you. In the same way a grown child or hired help might take dear old Dad or the boss to court, anybody who feels their settlement is ready for incorporation and an elected mayor and city council can petition the county or, failing that, a higher court."

Before he could go into more detail, seeing she had him up to the occasion again, Magnolia rolled atop him to skewer her shapely frame on an erection to be proud of and Longarm wondered why he'd ever wondered about the way you ran a shitty little railroad stop as she bounced up and down, this time with her heels on the floor and her tawny torso tilted back as she braced her weight with her hands gripping just above his knees.

Under the harsher light of a photographic studio the view might have been bawdy as a French postcard in motion. But the softer glow from the bedside candlestick made her look more romantic, if athletic, as she got to moving faster and faster, let out a kicked-pup whimper, and fell backward with her far flung hair between his bare toes, *her* bare toes stuck in his ears, and his poor old organ grinder fixing to break off inside her until he propped himself up with his elbows locked, just in time.

It felt way better, if not as bawdy, once they were at it old-fashioned, with him on top, and if they busted the cot, they busted the cot.

But they never did. Army cots were made to take abuse, albeit not exactly the sort the stretched canvas had to stand up to as a strong man set out to drive a shapely ass clean through it.

Longarm was too polite to say it, but he knew they were both starting to show off by the time good old Magnolia, having come eight times, wistfully remarked there just wasn't enough room on one army cot for two consenting adults to sleep on.

Longarm asked what she might sleep on in her own quarters.

She sighed and said, "A regular four-poster, of course. Had I wanted to go back to sleeping on the ground I'd have gone back to the reservation when my man's mount rolled on him. But I've a maid-of-all-work who comes by at dawn or earlier. She's a bitty white-trash orphan who's afraid I might fire her. So she works so hard to please me

52

I may have to fire her and, well, I don't want her catching me in bed with boarders."

Longarm said he followed her drift as Magnolia gathered her shift off the floor and slipped it back on. He didn't see how he was ever going to get it up again in any case. But as she rose from his side Magnolia sighed and said, "Oh, *tachesli*, I'm the boss and what do I care what a *winchacha wasichu* thinks about me? Grab your stuff and follow me. The night is young, I'm still hot and I want to *wachipi* some more!"

So, lest she take him for a sissy, they wound up in her wall-papered and frilly curtained bed chamber halfway around the inward-facing balcony and, when he consulted his pocket watch while hanging things up more tidy, he saw to his surprise it was barely past ten P.M.

That was still way too late to go calling on anyone else. They might be playing cards in the back rooms of more than one saloon at that hour, but the wise money was on calling it a night and as Magnolia shucked her shift again and dove into her four-posted featherbed ahead of him he couldn't come up with any *better* place to be at that hour.

So he gave her notion a try and damned if she didn't inspire a man to rise to the occasion, after all, kissing him balls and all as she hummed like a bumblebee.

He still had a time getting it back in her; it wasn't as stiff as before but a tad bigger—soft, she said—than her tight little ring-dang-doo was used to servicing.

But they finally got it back in, working together with two pillows under her firm brown rump, and after that it just naturally seemed to savvy it was expected to stand at attention in the presence of a lady.

So they were going at it like old pals, white style, when the night outside was rent by a fusillade of pistol shots so close they made the air inside tingle. As Longarm snuffed the bedside candle and rolled out and off Magnolia the floor beneath his bare feet twanged in time with the thuds of other feet, running down those outside stairs in high-heeled boots!

"Stay put! I'll find out!" Longarm whispered as he rose to grab for his hanging six-gun and follow it outside, bare-foot and bare ass if he had a hope in hell of catching shit.

He never did. As he got out on the balcony he could hear the echoes of those same boot heels tearing out of the courtyard to parts unknown and, worse yet, doors and windows were popping open all around. So he ducked back inside to start getting dressed in the dark, saying, "Going to have some company, directly. You'd best dress, too, and let me do the talking."

On their way downstairs, Longarm had time for a look-see where he would have been bedded down if a certain lack of virtue hadn't been its own reward. Gun smoke still hung sulfersome in the open doorway of his dark hired room. Standing in the doorway, Longarm saw he could just make out the dim form of that army cot until he struck a match and whistled at the ripped-up canvas he and Magnolia had tortured earlier.

Leading her down the stairway he muttered, "So much for discretion. Our high-heeled boy with what sounded like a double-action was told or figured out where I'd bed down after they missed me, earlier. He waited 'til he figured everyone was off the streets for the night and you were there when he paid us a late-night visit!"

She said, "Custis, I'm scared! What if they come back?"

He said, "Sounded like he was working alone. Nobody is after you. Just don't say nothing to trip me up as I try to confuse 'em some more."

So they were waiting downstairs with their clothes on when Uncle Roy and a whole lot of Sioux Siding came boiling into the courtyard, all of them asking what had happened at the same time.

Longarm told Uncle Roy, "I was fixing to ask you the same thing. I was helping Miss Magnolia, here, close down and tidy up for the night when we heard somebody emptying his wheel out here, somewheres. Sounded close."

The older lawman said, "Luke Waters from just across the way allows he saw somebody running out that archway waving a six-gun."

Longarm answered easily, "Do tell? I said the shots sounded close. We were in the kitchen at the time. Don't see how he could have been shooting at *us*."

Turning to Magnolia, he asked in an innocently curious tone, "Might you have anybody else boarding or residing on these premises, ma'am?"

Magnolia stifled a laugh of surprise and managed to reply there'd been nobody else upstairs or down but the two of them and added in a graver tone she meant to look around up yonder and make sure they hadn't been visited by a mighty noisy burglar while she washed and he dried.

As she lit out for her own quarters up the stairs, Uncle Roy asked a sneaky question. He asked Longarm, "What can you tell us about that other gun play down by the Western Union?"

Longarm asked, "Should I know something about other gun play?"

Uncle Roy said, "You should. Western Union's night clerk says you sent a night letter just a few minutes before somebody fired a buffalo rifle half the length of Market Street. Punctured a water trough north of Miss Zenobia's tea room and palm reading establishment."

Longarm shrugged and conceded, "Oh, *that* gunplay? Sounded like some kid set off a cherry bomb somewhere in the night. I never paid much mind to a little noise and no harm done."

The local law said, "You should have. You being a peace officer and harm being done. Around the time you were getting off that night letter somebody conked poor old Peg Leg Ferris on his poor old head and knocked him out cold while he was doing his job, lighting street lamps just up the way."

Longarm whistled and said, "My momma done told me not to jump at easy conclusions. Is the old lamplighter all right?"

Uncle Roy shrugged and replied, "He was crippled up to begin with. The doc says he ought to be back on his one foot in a day or so. So exactly where were you when that . . . cherry bomb went off?"

Longarm said, "Now that I think back I did notice some of the street lamps along Market Street were out. The detonation took place behind my back. Somewhere between the Western Union and the railroad stop farther south."

He saw that Scotch poet had been right about the tangled webs we weave when first we practice to deceive when Uncle Roy decided, "No offense, but I'd feel better if you'd sign a deposition to all of the above in front of Judge Boswell."

Longarm swallowed some and asked, "You got your own *judge* up here in Sioux Siding?"

Their town law snorted. "Well, sure we do. Did you take Sioux Siding for one of them shanty towns run half-ass off the cuff?"

"The thought never crossed my mind." Longarm soberly replied.

Chapter 7

The sworn depositions were taken by the Honorable Hamish Boswell, J.P. in the back room of the Warbonnet Saloon. Longarm never asked anybody why. Magnolia had told him earlier that the gravelly bearded Bowell owned the saloon, a feed store and the Sunset Livery near her beanery. The *J.P.* on the end gave the game away, albeit in Boswell's case he didn't claim to be the only law west of the pecos who let pals off for killing Chinamen when he couldn't find a law against killing Chinamen in his tome of Texas statutes. Judge Boswell seemed to savvy *J.P.* stood for Justice of the Peace.

A justice of the peace was the low man on the totem pole of the lower county courts. As such he had the power to levy modest fines or remand anybody who disturbed the peace to a higher court but the most awful thing he could do to any man was marry him up lawful before he sobered up.

That morning His Honor was out to gather a sheaf of depositions about all that gun play the night before and pass them on to the county seat a day's ride north. So he was seated at the card table with the modest back room overcrowded with his inner circle and the many less distinguished residents of Sioux Siding who'd offered suggestions to Uncle Roy about the directions those mysterious shots might have come from.

Longarm was mildly bemused to note Bram Drew wasn't there to cover the formalities for his paper until he recalled what the kid had confessed to him about having to stick type for their hand press every other day. As the tedium wore on, Longarm reflected that Bram Drew wasn't missing much.

Whether they were acting in good faith or out to pull a fast one, neither His Honor nor the fussy little CPA he'd enlisted as his court clerk knew all that much about the law. As each witness stepped up to the plate the clerk took down his deposition or sworn statement in shorthand, which was lawful enough. Then he had each witness sign his name on a blank sheet of typing paper, to be transcribed later in legible form, which was not.

No sworn statement was binding unless the one who'd signed it, as well as at least two witnesses, had *read* what they were signing first. For to swear in front of witnesses that you were signing a blank sheet of paper was comical, until one considered how easy it might be to fill in a bill of sale or a full confession to murder, rape and arson over said signatures.

But sometimes it could be smart to play dumb and give a sneak enough rope. So when it came his turn, Longarm went along with whatever they were up to.

Aware he was under oath, if they were on the level, Longarm was just as aware one or more of the skunks who'd been shooting at him could be there in the back room with the rest of the boys. So he chose his words with care to depose he had indeed heard what sounded like a cherry bomb or buffalo rifle down by the Western Union and left out some ducking and weaving. He allowed he had indeed heard what sounded like six rapid-fire shots from what might have been a pistol, up to the other end of Market Street in the vicinity of the Municipal Corral, leaving Magnolia's place out entire, and then he willingly signed the blank sheet his simple truth might or not wind up on.

He knew it would be a bother if they tried to change his deposition to a confession. He knew it would be evidence he, Billy Vail and their Uncle Sam would read as the confession of a stupidly crooked J.P. So what the hell.

After His Honor adjourned his hearing into the taproom for a belly-up, Longarm had one shot to show he was a sport and discreetly slipped out the back way as if to take a leak, then he just kept going. For it was going on ten A.M. and nothing he nor anyone had said that morning had told anybody a thing they hadn't already known about the night before.

So Longarm legged it some to make up for the time the shooter or more had gained on them all as the sign nobody had cut got ever harder to read.

Cherokee Adare's rival blacksmiths, Gonar Thorsen and Abel Weiss, both claimed to shoe half again as many hooves as a breed who spent that much of his own time in a saloon. So a little under two hundred men in town and closer to five hundred spread out across the surrounding range seemed as sensible a rough guess as Longarm felt he really needed.

Only one man at a time had pulled a trigger behind Ed Pitcairn and even if somebody else was shooting at *him*, Longarm knew he couldn't have seven hundred suspects gunning for him.

Having noticed nobody from the railroad had shown up that morning in the back room of the Warbonnet, Longarm trudged over to the dispatch shed by the tracks, where he found an older gent of the Dutch persuasion willing enough to talk, but not having a lot to say about anything clear of the Union Pacific right-of-way. The old railroader took the ruling of his little roost as seriously as if Queen Victoria had knighted him or as if he'd fathered every one of his modest crew.

He allowed any trash—white or stinking Indian—who stole so much as a lump of coal from the trackside tipple or pissed on a single cross-tie of his section would do so at mortal peril, but added he didn't give a fig about what went on off railroad property.

He said he and the dozen-odd employees who manned the switches or fed coal and water to company engines had heard the one nearby rifle shot and heard about other pistol shots in the dark to the north, but insisted he'd not only written them off as cow-town bullshit, himself, but instructed his crew and the few dependents the U.P. provied housing for not to ask around town.

He said, "We serve a witches brew of cattle men and sheep men, the free rangers and the fence-stringing homesteaders, mining men, lumber men, the tourist herders who want the mountains and forests left as they were and, in short, all sorts of troubled folk, red, white, black and every mix you can come up with."

He spat and added, "With every man jack of them as willing to buy them a rail ticket or ship most anything by rail. So we just can't afford to take sides and it's best not to know when there are sides to be taken!"

"Then there has been trouble up this way?" Longarm asked.

To which the old-timer flatly replied, "Not along the U.P. right-of-way. Railroad property used to extend a mile to the north and half a mile each way along the tracks from here. But the company sold its grant off a city lot at a time, and if they sold whole blocks of it to untidy neighbors it was their property to do with as they saw fit and I just work here. My job is to ease the east-west flow of company rolling stock through this section. They don't pay me to side with one set of potential passengers or the other."

Longarm allowed he followed the older man's drift and they shook to part friendly. The old-timer had told an experienced canvasser more than he might have intended to. He'd confirmed by his unwillingness to talk about the local power structure that there could be trouble in the offing.

Recalling what that younger newspaper man had bragged about knowing most everyone and everything around Sioux Siding, Longarm legged it on north to the storefront entrance of the *Sioux Siding News and Advertiser*. Once inside he could see at a glance they'd divided the interior with a wall-to-wall counter into a front business office and only slightly bigger pressroom.

A big blonde in an ink-stained smock of ecru sailcloth was sticking type as Longarm bellied up to their counter. She held on to the "Stick" or sliding metal type holder in her feminine albeit large left hand as she came over to shake with her right and declare herself Katrinka Ralston, the widow of the late Tex Ralston who'd founded the *Sioux Siding News and Advertiser*. She seemed quietly steamed about something else as she asked what she might do for him. After that she spoke English plain as any other country-schooled Midwestern gal and Longarm felt no call to ask if her elders had been Dutch or Scandahoovian. It seemed safe to assume they'd been something big and blond in their old country. Katrinka stood tall as Longarm and average-sized drunks were forever asking him how the weather was up yonder. But provided a man was not afraid of heights or a firm jaw, she was pretty as a China doll with big blue eyes a thirsty man might want to drown in. He admired the way she'd made a sort of crown for herself with those long blond braids across the top of her skull, too.

He explained who he was and why he wanted a word with Bram Drew, if he was handy. The boss lady Bram worked for said, "Bram hasn't come in yet and if he doesn't show up soon he needn't come in at all! I hired him to stick type when he wasn't scouting up something to go with our advertising and he'd not only left me with a dozen galleys to set but unwashed type in the wrong boxes! He's supposed to wash broken type in naptha before putting it back the way he damnit found it."

"Good help is hard to find, these days." Longarm nodded with the usual weary smile before he asked if she knew where her irresponsible printer, reporter or what-all might be found when he wasn't at work.

She wrinkled her pert nose and replied, "Shacked up with that Shanty drab he introduces as his wife after taking her away from a life of washing other men's laundry, I suppose. They share a dust-covered cottage over on D Street to the east. Across from the Baptist church. Number 448, I think. If you're anxious enough to walk that far with high noon coming on, tell him not to bother coming in at all unless he has a damned good excuse!"

Longarm started to point out that her cub reporter had been up late to cover the gun play up at Magnolia's the night before. Then he recalled Bram Drew hadn't been there, after the sounds of pistol shots had brought all those others from near and far.

He knew the buxom Katrinka had to know as much or more about her own surroundings as anybody working for her. But young Bram had established himself as a born gossip who volunteered more than he was asked, so Longarm allowed he'd go see what might have made the kid so late for work and she asked him to come back and tell her if Bram was down with some ague.

The sun was high and there was no wind near the center of the mushroom. So Longarm was cussing Miss Lemonade Lucy Hayes, the first lady who never served liquor at state banquets and made her own man wear a suit and tie in high summer, by the time he found the mustard-colored and sure enough dusty-looking little four room frame cottage across from the whitewashed Baptist church.

The dooryard grass had been neatly and recently mowed and somebody had planted a rosebush, which could have used more watering, near the front door. There was no front porch. You just stood on the cinder walk and knocked. But after he'd done so a spell, and nobody had come, Longarm tried the brass knob and it turned out they hadn't locked their front door, whether they'd gone out or not. So he opened the door, gave a holler, and went in.

The place was a mess. There were scattered papers across the floor and a bentwood chair had been knocked down and never helped back up. The floor could have done with some sweeping, even before the apparent stampede.

Calling out again, he found his way to the bedroom. The one chest of drawers stood with all but one drawer pulled halfway open and gaping empty. The one that wasn't lay across the bare mattress of the brass bedstead.

A jar of jam lay busted on the kitchen floor. Two place settings and what looked to be the leftovers of a supper still occupied the kitchen table. The cottage wasn't big enough to call for a dining room.

Lighting a three-for-a-nickel cheroot thoughtfully, Longarm told the match as he was shaking it out, "The question before the house is whether Bram Drew and his gal moved out sudden but willing, or whether they were drug out kicking and screaming by a person or persons unknown."

Going out the back door, he spied a next-door neighbor woman taking in some sun-dried laundry and, being there was no fence dividing the two backyards, Longarm got rid of the smoke and fished out his badge to flash in peace as he strode on over to join her by her clothesline.

Introducing himself as he put his badge and ID away with his wallet, Longarm asked if she could tell him when the Drews, next door, might have hauled out.

She said she hadn't even known they were gone and, when pressed, felt sure she'd have noticed had anybody been hauled away by a lynch mob just before or after dark. She agreed with Longarm that even a sloppy house-wife cleared the table by bedtime, even if she left the dishes in the sink for later. So Longarm settled on any time between sundown and midnight as the hour of their departure. When the older woman speculated on a sneak-out on their landlord Longarm felt no call to point out Bram Drew had a steady job or that it wasn't all that close to the first of the month. For he figured the less anybody gossiped the less bullshit he'd be tripping over as he worked on . . . what?

Where in the U.S. Constitution did it say an ambitious young newspaper man with mayhaps a nagging woman might not suddenly see fit to try for a better job up or down the U.P. Line?

Thanking the neighbor lady with a tick of his hat brim, Longarm decided to retrace his steps to that dispatch shed and see if his new pal who ran the section could offer any help with that question.

The railroad had its own telegraph wires strung along-side their right-of-way and to board a night train out in either direction, the missing couple would have had to mention their intentions to the local dispatcher or the con-ductor of said train. Seeing it looked as if they'd hauled out with a heap of personal belongings, Longarm was betting on the dispatcher. Nobody boarded a train at any hour with a whole lot of baggage unless they had a little help. But by the time Longarm saw the sun-silvered open platform of the the lonesome stop ahead of him he was commencing to feel like that poor headless chicken running around in circles, dad blast Bram Drew or whoever might have frog marched him off through the gathering dusk on the sneak!

As he got to the foot of the north-south D Street and turned toward the not-too-distant dispatch shed on his side of the water tower, Longarm was hailed from back the way he'd come and turned to see two riders dressed in matching navy blue shirts and black Stetsons with high Texican crowns as well as tied-down holsters, and neither was smiling as they strode in step to join him there on the sun-baked dust and dung of D Street.

The more lean and hungry looking of the pair said, "We've been looking for you all over town, Longarm. You sure do get around on them long legs of your'n."

Longarm said, "That's what they pay me for and since you've caught up with me at last, what can I do for you, Mr. . . . ?"

"Walsh. They call me Waco Walsh," the obvious Texican replied, adding, "I am the ramrod for the Rocking H. I ride for Miss Maureen Flannery and she was not at all pleased when Chinks Potter rode in with a fat lip and a tale of being rawhided by a notorious gunslick. So you can see how it has to be, Notorious Gunslick."

Longarm smiled thinly and softly asked, "Nope. I'm waiting for you to tell me how it has to be, Mr. Walsh."

The foreman of the Rocking H exchanged glances with his armed and just as dangerous looking sidekick before he grinned wolfishly and declared, "You sure must enjoy living dangerous, Denver Boy!"

To which Longarm could only reply, "That's another thing they pay me for. So I await your pleasure, Texas Boy."

Chapter 8

A million mighty tense years went by. Then Waco Walsh laughed easily and joshed, "Don't talk like a fool kid, Longarm. You know full well me and old Trevor here ain't about to shoot it out in the middle of town in the middle of the day with a federal lawman!"

"I did notice somebody with more sand in his craw and less brag in his talk pegged a shot at me over on Market Street after dark last night," said Longarm with a wolfish smile of his own.

Waco Walsh said, "That wasn't anybody off the Rocking H. You'll *know* who's after you if Miss Maureen tells us to clean your plow. Me and old Trevor here just wanted to save both you and Miss Maureen some trouble. I was about to suggest, before you got your bowels in an uproar, it might be best if you was to just agree to live and let live."

"How do I go about that?" asked Longarm, dryly.

Waco said, "I told Miss Maureen I'd run you out of Sioux Siding to save her the bother and possible legal fees. Man to man as well as off to one side, I'd look just as good and you wouldn't look no worse if you was to just quit while we're both ahead. I mean, board yourself a train out and save us all a whole lot of trouble."

Longarm chuckled and said, "I pulled that off at a dance one night. This pretty little thing was all excited about remarks a good old boy had passed. So I got him off to one side and asked him polite if he'd be as willing to avoid the fight as me. So we shook on it, he lit out, and later on that night I got laid."

"Ain't nothing like that going on between Miss Maureen and me!" Waco protested with convincing indignation, whether sincere or not, and added, "Miss Maureen is more like a big sister or a doting aunt to fat-lipped Chinks Potter as well. That's how come you're in more trouble than you seem willing to face. I don't *want* to fight you, Longarm. I'm a grown man and I know better. But I ride for a boss lady with a whim of iron and come Saturday night or even earlier, she'll be riding in with the boys after paying them off and—"

"The Rocking H pays by the week instead of the month?" Longarm cut in, adding, "This boss lady of yours must enjoy bookkeeping a heap as well. For I got to herd cows for many an outfit before I went to work for the justice department and bless my soul if any of them paid me more often than at the end of the month, if then."

He reached for another smoke as he added thoughtfully, "This one boss held off on paying toad squat before we drove his herd all the way up to Dodge and even then the son of a bitch tried to screw us fifty cents on the dollar."

Waco shrugged and said, "All right. You caught me in a fib. I was only trying to impress it on your ass that come this time tomorrow night you could find yourself up against an Irish temper and more than two dozen young waddies showing off for her, with six-guns!"

Longarm allowed he was glad Waco and old Tevor

weren't showing off in front of anybody and added he had beeswax of his own to tend to. So they just stood there like big-ass birds when he turned his back on them and walked away. They might or might not have noticed he could see them both reflected in the plate glass window of a ladies notions shop until he was out of easy pistol range. But in truth he hadn't expected either to draw on his back. Waco had already pointed out how awkward such a shooting might be to explain.

The way friendlier dispatcher, once Longarm caught up with him again, was able to establish neither Bram Drew nor his common-law laundress had left Sioux Siding the night before by rail.

When he pointed out there was no natural nor manmade law saying a young couple and all their belongings couldn't head most any direction by wagon across wide open short-grass range, Longarm sighed and said, "I sure wish that wasn't so true. My boss, Marshal Vail, calls what I'm trying to do a process of elimination. But, so far, I haven't eliminated one suspect in the killing of Ed Pitcairn and, as you just said, I can't tell whether my missing newspaper man and his woman left willingly or not, east, west, north, south or up in smoke if the goblins got 'em!"

The older man laughed and asked if that was where Frank and Jesse might have gone since the law lost track of them after the Northfield Raid.

Longarm shrugged and said, "Ain't sure I believe in the goblins coming for wicked children like some say. But some wicked children surely vanish into thin air, forever, as if the goblins got 'em."

Then, on reflection, he felt obliged to add, "I don't know about his reformed laundress, but Bram Drew never struck me as wicked enough to be on the dodge from the law. I'm still workig on whether they might have owed enough money to call for mysterious late night move-outs."

So they shook again and Longarm headed back to the *Sioux Siding News and Advertiser* to see what the missing newspaper man's boss might be able to tell him about that.

Along the way, Uncle Roy Sanderson fell in beside him to ask where he was headed *now*, adding, "What did Waco Walsh and Trevor Klein want with you earlier?"

Longarm said, "I'm headed for where Bram Drew used to work. Has anybody told you he seems to be missing?"

Uncle Roy replied, "Him and his doxie ain't missing. They skipped out on three months' rent and their landlord was mad as hell about that when he came in to press charges this morning. Let's get back to your run-in with them two Rocking H riders."

Longarm snorted and said, "Wasn't a run-in. I just called a bully boy's bluff."

As they trudged in step under the afternoon sun, Longarm added, "I used to be afraid of bully boys when I was a little boy. I have never cottoned to the breed since I got big enough to push back. That she-male bully both of them ride for seems to be trying to bluff me into running for it, too. Old Waco warned me she'll be riding in with a dozen or more guns to scare this child and make him cry."

Uncle Roy sounded serious as he said, "I follow your drift about most bullies, Longarm. But Maureen Flannery is the real deal. They say that when she caught up with the Comanche who scalped her man, she shot him in both knees and elbows to render him helpless as she sat on his chest with her dead lover's bowie to scalp the crippled-up Indian, alive!"

"They say there's this wonderous critter called the hoop snake," Longarm replied, going on to add, "They

70

say it sticks its tail in its mouth to roll like a hoop, faster than a locomotive, and have I failed to mention the fabulous monster said to haunt the Jersey Pine Barrens?"

Uncle Roy protested, "Hold on. I never said Maureen Flannery was exactly a monster. I said she was inclined to *act* like one when you got her riled."

Longarm shrugged and said, "I haven't done anything a man or woman with a lick of sense would get that riled about. One of her cowhands started up with me and wound up with a fat lip. Is that any sensible reason to run a lawman on duty out of here?"

Uncle Roy replied, "Would I be worried if I thought Maureen Flannery had a lick of sense? You ain't the first stranger to cross her, Longarm. I just hate it when they send somebody over from the county seat, asking how come I haven't arrested her or any of her hands."

"Why haven't you arrested her or any of her hands?" asked Longarm.

Uncle Roy sighed and said, "Because I feel I'm too young to die. We are talking about a wild woman who took on the Comanche Nation one time, and won!"

Longarm let it go. If Uncle Roy was too ignorant to know how Sheriff Peppin of Lincoln County had simply called on the ninth Cavalry out of nearby Fort Stanton when he felt the Tunstall-McSween faction was too tough for him and his county law to handle he was a piss poor excuse just playing at enforcing toad squat.

Sioux Siding's excuse for town law didn't tag along all the way back to the newspaper office. So Longarm could tell Katrinka Ralston in private why she was sticking type all by herself that afternoon.

The big buxom blonde sounded worried as she said, "Bram could have come to me if he was in trouble with Jubel Stark. I'd have advanced him enough to cover the little he could have owed the old skinflint!"

Longarm said, "If we're talking about Bram's landlord, he claims the kid owed him for three months on that cottage."

"At fifteen dollars a month," Katrinka replied, adding, "that comes to less than a month's salary when you add it all up and how do we know Bram owed anybody anything? How do we know Bram and his drab left *willingly*? How do we know they weren't . . . abducted?"

Longarm decided, "That's possible, Miss Katrinka. But it gets tougher to swallow when you consider how often kidnappers take along their victim's personal baggage. Neighbor lady allows they left quiet as them Arabs in that poem who silently folded their tents and slipped away."

She insisted, "He'd have told me if he was in a jam for money. He has in the past. So he knew I was good for an advance, just as I knew he was willing to work at half pay until we worked it out. We were *friends*, ah, Custis. I can't think of any reason Bram might have for leaving without one word to me."

Longarm sighed and said, "Neither can I. Like Miss Alice said when she wound up in Wonderland, things just keep getting curiouser and curiouser in these parts! They send me up this way to look into what sounded like a simple back shooting and . . . You know, that's mighty curious, too!"

She asked what he meant, moving down the counter to open a panel and invite him in back for some whistle wetting filed under gin.

As he followed her back Longarm explained, "The trail of Ed Pitcairn's killer was colder than a banker's heart before I ever got up here. The scene of the crime was a well-traveled thoroughfare with hoofprints and worse erasing any sign poor Pitcairn had died there. Your local law told me he and his deputies had canvassed in vain for witnesses. My home office is of the opinion Pitcairn lied

72

about his reasons for heading up this way to be killed by someone who was expecting him. He had, in sum, conspired in his own murder by leaving us nothing to go on. So had things gone as they usually go when they send this child on a snipe hunt, I'd have been packing it in about now and heading back to Denver to file the backshooting of Ed Pitcairn in our Maybe Someday file."

She poured them both heroic tumblers of sloe gin, bless her she-male tastes, as she allowed that hadn't struck her as all that curious.

He said, "I'd have been thinking about leaving Sioux Siding by now if only they'd have let me *be*! But it makes a lawman pure curious when they commence to peg shots at him and try to scare him into leaving in other curious ways. For, like I said, the trail was cold, or it sure *felt* cold, before folks around here commenced to act as if I might be getting warm!"

As they stood between the files and hand press, sipping the sloe gin like sorority sisters, Longarm tersely filled the newspaper gal in on his recent misadventures, leaving out the part about Magnolia Epworth, but asked her to sit on the story in exchange for an exclusive, once he figured what in blue blazes he was really working on.

He added, "Somebody may be putting Maureen Flannery and her Rocking H riders up to it. But Chinks Potter had no call to start up with me and after that neither his outfit nor their boss lady had call to run me out of here. After that we have to consider Bram Drew leaving so sudden in a unannounced manner."

Katrinka proved she had a nose for news by suggesting, "As if Bram was getting warm, or might have spilled something they didn't want spilled to a stranger with a badge. I think I know who might be pulling strings from his high and mighty land and loan office, the old spider."

Longarm asked who they were talking about.

She said, "Jubel Stark. Present company excepted, most everyone in Sioux Siding jumps when Jubel Stark pulls their strings. Most everyone in Sioux Siding *owes* Jubel Stark."

Longarm started to ask a dumb question. He saved her a heap of breath by just recalling how most every small town across the land had a Jubel Stark who'd gotten there first with a bankroll to wheel and deal in land and mortgages on the same. Katrinka had just said the cuss ran his own loan office as well as his real estate operation. Uncle Roy Sanderson had never said Jubel Stark had been the name of the landlord charging Bram Drew with skipping out on his rent. Bram's boss, Katrinka, had.

It was easy to politely but firmly refuse a second pouring of girlish gin. So Katrinka poured another for herself as she decided, "That Deputy Pitcairn they murdered must have been about to expose some secret serious enough to die for. They don't want you uncovering it. So they've run Bram and that girl, I think her name's Kitty, out of Sioux Siding, I hope. Your point about all that missing baggage is a straw worth grasping for. I *like* Bram, and poor drab Kitty has never done anything to me."

She knocked back her drink, without a chaser, as one could manage with sloe gin after the first few shots, and asked, "But what could the secret be, and what are you going to do now?"

Longarm said, "Might be more than one secret, starting with the holds Jubel Stark or somebody worse could be holding over any number. After that I'm still working on my next best move. So far, I've been running around like a decapitated chicken with everybody watching me. Don't see how I'm supposed to uncover any secrets with everybody watching me."

They both fell into silent thought as, off in the distance, the whistle of an approaching locomotive announced the afternoon westbound was running a little early.

As the sad but oddly tempting wail faded away Longarm smiled wistfully and asked, "Ain't it a caution how, no matter what you may be up to, that wistful invitation makes you want to drop whatever you're up to and run off by rail to strange sounding places you've never really studied on?"

She sighed and said, "Every night, when the eastbound passes through, reminding me I've never seen New York City, London Town or Paris, France. What if everyone here in Sioux Siding thought you'd given in to temptation and boarded that westbound, Custis? What if, after it pulled out, you were nowhere to be seen on the streets of Sioux Siding?"

He started to say he wasn't ready to give up. Then Longarm smiled at her to ask, "Are you suggesting I *hide out* as that westbound leaves for Cheyenne?"

She grinned back to say, "Why not? Who'd be watching you pussy-foot in the dark after sundown if they thought you were in Cheyenne this evening?"

He asked where she had it in mind for him to lay so low.

She answered, simply, "Right upstairs, in my quarters. You don't even have to step outside while that westbound stops to jerk water and, for all we know, steam on with you on board, you sneaky thing!"

Chapter 9

Katrinka's spur-of-the-moment plan was only reckless until you studied on it. Once you studied on it, it had the virtues of simplicity as well as the unexpected.

Longarm had been told to leave and in turn told everybody to go fuck themselves. So nobody in Sioux Siding had much call to be *watching* for him when that early afternoon varnish paused just long enough to take on water, drop off a mail bag and take the same aboard.

For those few minutes along the siding, postal and railroad workers would be milling back and forth and unless someone with no business down along the tracks was keeping a tally on bodies getting on and off, who was to say just who might have gotten on or off, after the train had rolled on out to the main line again?

Longarm had no baggage to worry him or anyone else as the big buxom blonde led him up her back stairs to the mighty spacious private quarters offered by the same space upstairs as her whole newspaper took up down below. Her digs were laid out in what they called a railroad flat back East where more folk lived in tenements, with one family piled atop another like cake layers. They called such a layout a railroad flat because rooms about the same size were strung out like boxcars, all opening on to one hallway along one side. She had the one to the rear appointed as her kitchen with an icebox and running water for her big kitchen sink and the sneaky bathtub built under a fold-up countertop. The shittery next to the kitchen had modern plumbing for its smaller sink and flush commode as well.

The next room forward had been meant as a dining room but Katrinka had set it up as a sort of studio where she worked on layouts at a big draftsman's table and composed copy at a typewriter that would have made old Henry, back at the Denver office, green with envy.

Best of all, the newspaper gal maintained a modest but tidy morgue of the more interesting articles she'd run downstairs. So Longarm had things to occupy his mind that afternoon. But first she led him all the way up front, where the lace curtains of the big old gal's big old bedroom overlooked D Street.

She sat him near the windows in a rocking chair with a pitcher of iced tea, seeing he wouldn't drink more sloe gin, and went back down to play an important part in their charade by getting busy in her pressroom some more.

Hence it came to pass, though neither of them could see it, that the westbound varnish rolled in and rolled out after a mild flurry along its length of eight passenger, dining and mail cars, along with the 4-4 engine and its tender, of course, while Longarm was going through the morgue and Katrinka stuck type down below and a third deputy in a row reported in to inform Uncle Roy they hadn't seen hide nor hair of that federal lawman since that westbound varnish pulled out.

Uncle Roy was bellied up to the bar in the Warbonnet at that hour and so Cherokee Adare was there to marvel,

"Do you reckon he left aboard that westbound, Uncle Roy?"

The older man replied, "Too early to say. I had McBride ask that U.P. dispatcher about that. The Dutchman couldn't say whether Longarm left aboard that particular train. But he did recall how old Longarm stopped by more than once earlier."

"Like a hound dog sniffing shy around a bitch in heat?" asked Cherokee.

Uncle Roy sipped some suds and decided, "Too early to say. He never went back to Widow Epworth's after she served him breakfast in bed this morning."

Cherokee scowled and demanded, "Who says Miss Magnolia did any such a thing this morning?"

The older man smiled knowingly and said, "Martinez has been fucking her cleaning woman. Martinez allows he'd much rather fuck Miss Magnolia, but none of us get to fuck all the gals we'd care to fuck, so—"

"Did Martinez say Miss Magnolia's been fucking Longarm?" the breed cut in with his gun hand hovering like a hawk near his Schofield .45.

Uncle Roy calmly replied, "Martinez wasn't there. The cleaning woman he gets to fuck only told him she carried the breakfast tray upstairs to where the lawman reclined in Miss Magnolia's bed chamber. Miss Magnolia being downstairs, slinging hash and scrambled eggs to morning customers at the time. So it's remotely possible she accommodated a paying guest whose original sleeping arrangements had been shot up the night before. Cleaning woman said the Army cot in that other room had been shot to shit and I'm still wondering why Longarm never saw fit to tell me or His Honor about that."

Cherokee asked, "Then it's as likely that . . . Creek gal slept in one of her other hired rooms on another Army cot after moving Longarm to a more comfortable bed, lest he move out on her?"

Uncle Roy said anything was possible but added that he had his doubts about a man with Longarm's reputation as a lady killer alone upstairs with any single lady.

Cherokee grumbled, "Aw, she ain't no lady. She's a fucking *Creek*!"

Uncle Roy laughed and said, "Don't try to teach your granny how to suck eggs or tell an old goat like me you ain't been jerking off regular in honor of Widow Epworth, and she's French and Osage. Martinez asked about that."

As if he'd heard his name mentioned, the dapper young Hernan Martinez came through the bat-wings, dressed Anglo in blue denim and looking mighty thirsty. As he bellied up to the bar with Uncle Roy the Mexican said he'd have anything wet and added, "That dick-head from Denver never went back to the widow's beanery and when I just now sauntered past that newspaper old Bram Drew used to work for that big blonde was working alone in the back."

As Mahoney slid a stein of needled beer across the zinc to him the Mexican added, "Oh, almost forgot. I scouted around that cottage like you asked and the lady next door says Longarm was there, earlier, asking for Bram and his Kitty."

Uncle Roy asked, "Could she tell whether Longarm had cut any sign next door, pard?"

Martinez inhaled some suds, sighed with relief, and replied, "I asked about that, right out, seeing she knew I was the law and had as much of a right to worry about missing reporters as any other lawman. But she tells me she got the impression Longarm left completely in the dark. So unless Longarm's sneaky as some say, neither Bram nor Kitty left any notes behind as they were being helped off the property with their baggage."

Cherokee said, "I'm missing something, Uncle Roy? Am I to understand that newspaper man was, ah, aided and abetted by anyone we know as they skipped out on the rent like Jubel Stark said?"

Uncle Roy sighed and said, "I've always admired a man who can think on his feet. So start thinking on your fucking *feet*, Cherokee!"

To which the younger breed felt obliged to answer, simply, "Oh, right."

Meanwhile, back at Katrinka's, Longarm was going through her morgue as she stuck type for all to see, alone, downstairs.

Left to his druthers, Longarm hated paperwork so hard he would have been more willing to track hogs through a canebreak on hands and knees than root for signs in dusty old newspaper clippings. But good old Henry, who liked to paw through the files in Longarm's home office, wasn't there to pull such a shit detail. So Longarm had to, making occasional notes in his aptly named notebook with a stub pencil as he gained a more detailed, if not noteworthy, picture of the way things worked around Sioux Siding.

Thanks to the whole shebang being so recently settled, and seeing the buxom widow of a founding father who'd covered the news fit to print in Sioux Siding from the beginning had already pointed it out, Longarm found it duck-soup simple to follow the meteoric rise of Jubel Stark, a hitherto undistinguished and middle-aged nobody much who'd wound up a mighty big frog in however small a puddle in a mighty short time.

Reading between the lines some, Longarm was able to see how old Jubel had bought a city block of railroad land on credit, run up a line of jerry built business frontage, and managed to rent or sell enough improved property to pay off the Union Pacific Land Office just as they were fixing to foreclose on his original mortgage. Longarm had read what J. Gould had said about the first million being the only really hard million to make.

Browsing through articles and advertising on the subject of real estate it was easy enough to see Jubel Stark had most everybody in Sioux Siding asking, "How high?" whenever he said, "Jump!" There was shit about their big frog chairing a meeting to determine one civic improvement or another, with old Jubel deciding pro or con no matter how the majority there might have voted. The late Tex Ralston and later both his widow and young Bram Drew had written sort of satiric articles about the way old Jubel always seemed to get his way. So Longarm wasn't the first to marvel about it out loud, muttering, "How? Near as I can tell, the old fart owns no more than half the place, outright. Can't everyone in Sioux Siding live in one of his rental properties or owe him money and . . . what the hell . . . ?"

One of Bram Drew's reports from earlier that very year related how Miss Maureen Flannery of the Rocking H had dismissed two of her riders, more in sorrow than in anger, after they'd gotten liquored up and ridden hard across the manicured lawns and flower beds of the Eldridge place, as one described a mansard-roofed frame mansion built, maintained, and granted fee simple to the widow of the late Doc Eldridge as a sort of inhabited shrine to her husband by, who else, the noteworty realtor, Jubel Stark!

Yet Uncle Roy had warned how Maureen Flannery had bailed Chinks Potter out and hushed things up after he'd shot a man's toe off? There was more to all this than met the casual eye. So, since that process of elimination started with plain old bullshit, Longarm dug through another drawer and then some to discover how, sure enough, Chinks Potter had indeed shot one Fred Zuber of Acme Hardware in the left foot, maiming him considerably and screaming for justice until . . . here it was almost a month later, old Fred decided to drop the charges and left both Wyoming and Acme Hardware as a wiser and more prosperous man.

Spitting paper dust as he resisted the temptation to smoke with all that paper dust swirling around him, Longarm dug deeper for more on the oddly more serious offense of offending a widow woman admired by old Jubel Stark. But as he dug back deeper he reluctantly decided the relationship sounded pure.

According to the obituary written by Katrinka's man before he'd up and died, himself, Doc Eldridge and his wife, Miss Stella, had been the first and for some time only medical facility in Sioux Siding. Their connection with Jubel Stark read innocent. He'd rented first a modest and later that imposing pile he'd built for himself to be used as combined quarters and a clinic, with the nearest regular hospital being in far-off Cheyenne.

Despite the cynical tone Tex Ralston had expressed in other items he'd penned about the self-made big-shot, he'd found no way to low-rate Jubel Stark for renting the way bigger house to the doc at the same rent, moving his own stuck-up self into an even grander mansion he'd erected just up F Street and, the doc dying of a heart-stroke less than two years later, the heart-sick widow's crusty landlord had signed the property over to her, lock stock and barrel, with the provision she recruit another doctor and hire the clinic out to him.

Tex Ralston hadn't been able to resist noting the chronic condition of some kind that Doc Eldridge had been treating old Stark for. But fair was fair and they did say Attila the Hun had been kindly to his horses. So it stood to reason a big-shot being treated regular by a doc he had admired might do right by the good old boy's widow, or take it serious when liquored-up cowhands upset her.

But it didn't stand to reason that a boss lady who'd fire hands just for upsetting folks without hurting them would go to bat for a born bully who'd shot an innocent man's toe off. So Longarm found himself nodding in agreement where Bram Drew who'd written both offenses up, intimated the interest of a puppet master in the first instance and a lack of interest in the second.

"So what hold might Jubel Stark have over Maureen Flannery and how can I get him to use it in my behalf?" Longarm asked the bundle of clippings spread like solitaire cards across Katrinka's desk and decided, "He has some hold on her. Strong enough to rein in a natural spitfire with the maternal instincts of a she-bear defending its cubs. But I'll be switched with snakes if you can read all about it in the newspapers!"

He got to work at what old Henry called cross-referals, digging out a lot less, but some items worth interest about the imperious Maureen Flannery and her budding cattle barony to the north. Her Rocking H shipped grass-fed beef in considerable, if uncertain, numbers at the end of every roundup and Riding H hands seemed to brush with other outfits every time everybody rode out to round up the widely scattered and free ranging beef. So Maureen Flannery should have been in serious debt to a puppet master with a moneybag hold over her. That left . . . what?

He hadn't found out hours later, when Katrinka came upstairs to tell him she'd put her next edition to bed. It was pushing suppertime, and so far nobody had come by to ask about him since that train passed through.

She'd shed her ink-stained smock and filled out the calico summer dress she'd been wearing under it more curvacious. He'd long since shucked his tweed coat and the sissy shoestring tie the current dress regulations had saddled him with. So he followed her back to her kitchen in his vest and shirtsleeves, albeit still wearing his six-gun in light of the uncertain times.

Katrinka seemed surprised and touched when he offered to help. In point of fact he did no more than get her coal-fired range going and then set the table as she fried up some pork chops and diced potatoes, having agreed with him on rabbit food when he demured to her offer of warmed-over beet tops.

But she would go on about how, even though she'd loved him dearly and missed him sore, her late Tex Ralston had never helped with the meals but seemed to feel it was only right he work at the desk in yonder while she did all the kitchen chores.

Longarm had never figured for certain why women insisted on telling a man about all the other men who'd used and abused them, while denying him the mere mention of any other woman he might have held hands with.

So she never heard a word about Roping Sally, Jessie Starbuck or that Long Island debutante who'd damn near convinced him it was time to settle down as Katrinka went on about never forgiving herself for not being in the mood the night her Tex had suddenly keeled over and died on her. Longarm found it more interesting that the doc who'd decided her man had overworked his fool self into a brain-stroke had been the one who'd replaced the late Doc Eldridge over on F Street.

He said as much, trying to get the conversation back to her newspaper morgue before she could say right out how often and in what position she and her poor dead dear had fornicated.

Katrinka said Bram Drew had covered the arrival and setting up shop of the new doctor in town. She didn't seem too interested. When he asked if she knew what Doc Eldrige and likely his succesor had been treating Jubel

Stark for she shrugged and said, "Most likely some social disease. They say the mean old thing dwells alone in his big spooky house and never seems to take any interest in women. So it's possible he's not up to taking interest in women. Or mayhaps he prefers boys. I understand some men are like that. I've never understood just what two boys, or two girls, could do to one another that would feel half so grand."

Longarm allowed he hadn't, either, and tried to steer them back to the mysterious hold the sort of spooky old cuss seemed to have on so many in and around Sioux Siding.

She suggested they talk about it up front, where they could watch the street as darkness fell and the Lord only knew what might happen next.

As they moved along the hallway, with Katrinka bringing along the sloe gin and a pitcher of ice shaved from the bigger block in her kitchen, Longarm found himself wondering how good old Magnolia was likely to take it when, not if, she discovered he'd spent the night under another gal's roof, no matter what the excuse, delivered with protestations of innocence. So he knew he was damned if he did and damned if he didn't as Katrinka sat him back down by the lace curtains with his six-gun and a tumbler of gin to hold the fort while she slipped into something more comfortable.

So he sipped sloe gin and watched the street out front as darkness fell and nobody seemed to be turning on any street lamps. Uncle Roy had said the one lamplighter in Sioux Siding would be laid up a spell.

So it was fairly dark, but not that dark, when Katrinka returned to announce she felt ever so much more comfortable, now.

Longarm couldn't say he felt all that comfortable when he turned to see over six feet of buxom blond in the doorway, naked as a jay but way more tempting.

Chapter 10

As Longarm rose to the occasion in every way and shucked his own duds while getting into bed with the buxom Katrinka, he decided the best tack to take with the dusky Magnolia would be Indian-style.

Indian gals were jealous as most others, but raised to be more practical than Queen Victoria among natural men who practiced polygamy and made no bones about it, holding that a natural man was neither supposed to lie to anybody nor restrict his natural feeling to one particular *wichincha*.

Longarm had to allow there was much to be said for such notions as he mounted a whole new experience who didn't need a pillow under her shapely but massive ass to welcome his first penetration all the way to the roots. And as they were getting to know each other in the Biblical sense indeed, somebody lit a street lamp out front, after all, to make Katrinka's milk-white tits almost glow in the dimly romantic light as they bobbed in time with their mutual thrusts. As in the case of that other lonesome widow on the north end of Market Street, Katrinka came ahead of him and proceeded to cry whilst he tried to catch up with her.

It wasn't easy. He knew better than to say anything as he threw the blocks to her and tried to kiss away her tears while she wiggled, jiggled and bawled. He feared from past experience he knew what he was in for once he stopped for breath. He cussed his own weak nature as he kept pounding away while the voice of reason told him to take it out and tell her he was sorry and that he'd never fuck her again.

It was the only way to score at least a partial victory when a horny gal who'd just had her wicked way with a man decided to blame it all on him and the liquor he'd forced on her.

It sounded tediously familiar, and as he was fixing to come, the big blonde gasped, "Oh, my lands, what are you *doing* to me?"

But then, as he was doing it indeed, Katrinka wrapped her big old arms and legs around him tight to sob, "I can't believe it! I'm going to come again and if you stop *now* I'll kill you!"

So he didn't stop and if she'd been winding up to accuse him of raping a helpless drunk she seemed to have gotten over the notion by the time she moaned, "Oh, that was lovely! Can I get on top when we do it again?"

He suggested they share a smoke and get their wind back first, seeing the night was so young and she fucked so fine.

She giggled and protested he was leading her into all sorts of temptations as she puffed on what she said was her first three-for-a-nickel cheroot in a manner suggesting she might be telling the truth. She never inhaled and coughed just the same, demanding he tell her why men smoked, now that she'd tried it.

Fondling one big bare tit as she snuggled her blond head on his bare shoulder, Longarm confessed, "I've often wondered as I lit a smoke at last after wanting one for hours. The first few drags seem to relieve some odd itch and then you barely taste anything and, if you study on it, you sort of wonder why you didn't spend the nickel on something like a beer or even a soda pop."

He took a deep drag, blew a thoughtful smoke ring, and remarked in a wistful tone, "It's as if you took a pretty gal dancing and then spent more showering her with flowers, books and candy, only to find out when you mounted her at last that nothing much happened after the first deep thrust."

She reached down to fondle his semi-erection as she volunteered to do all the work and assured him she expected something to happen. So he got rid of the cheroot, Katrinka got on top and what happened was that he felt it down to his toes when he shot another wad up into all those pneumatic charms and then, of course, had to get on top with an elbow hooked under a knee to either side as he took charge of his own destiny again.

By the time he'd come thrice, since he was only human, Katrinka protested she was only human, hadn't been getting any lately, and felt sort of raw down yonder. But at least she wasn't crying and never said the man she'd invited to spend the night with her had taken cruel advantage of a poor weak-natured widow woman. So now, if only he could get Magnolia to be such a pal, or, better yet, keep her from finding out before he could get the hell out of Sioux Siding. . . .

"That reminds me." He sighed, rolling off to reach for that snuffed cheroot and then forget about it as he continued, "Ed Pitcairn must have been killed to keep his private mission up this way a secret. Bram Drew and his Kitty may have been run off, or worse, because you had him out on the streets, every other day, gathering all the news that was fit to print and, for all we know, stumbling over secrets nobody wanted in a newspaper, or mayhaps the county clerk's files."

Katrinka shuddered in his arms, an awesome feeling, and asked him if he thought her young reporter and printer's devil had been run out or kidnapped.

Longarm said, "Kidnappers hardly ever give a victim time to pack just about everything he owns. I suspect the furniture they left behind goes with the rented cottage. I mean to ask Jubel Stark when I get the chance."

She gasped, "You mean to confront Jubel Stark, knowing he's more than likely the master sneak behind all your troubles, dear?"

Longarm replied, "I ain't the one in trouble. The rascal who killed or ordered the killing of a federal deputy is the one in trouble. I'm just another federal deputy somebody's out to discourage or kill and I don't know Jubel Stark is that somebody."

She asked how come, in that case, Longarm wanted to question the sort of spooky old cuss.

He said, "For openers, he *could* be that somebody and after that I'd like to know what makes him so spooky. From what I've noticed in person up this way as well as digging through your morgue, folks here in Sioux Siding can be divided into those who don't seem to give a hang about old Jubel and those who seem scared skinny of him."

She asked for examples.

He said, "For openers, neither you, yourself, nor your Bram Drew, up until recently, seem or seemed at all afraid of the big frog in your little puddle, no offense. I've met others, a railroad dispatcher and another . . . widow woman running her own business in these parts, who hardly seemed to know Jubel Stark was there."

She asked, "Why should anyone who wasn't renting or borrowing money off him?"

He said, "That's what I mean. Why should they? Yet from articles I've just read he must have the boys in the back room at the Warbonnet, from Boswell and Uncle Roy Sanderson down to their part-time deputies and . . . hold on, who bopped Peg Leg Ferris on the head if Jubel Stark wanted all those street lamps out? A man who has the men who run Sioux Siding dancing to his tune could have simply ordered old Ferris not to light the lamps down by the Western Union, right?"

Katrinka proved she was a born newspaper woman by pointing out, "Unless they wanted you to think what you just thought. Two can keep a secret if one of them is dead, and would you let an old windy drunk such as Peg Leg Ferris know you were plotting to shoot a federal deputy in the back if you didn't have to?"

Longarm snuggled her closer and declared, "I admire women wiser in the ways of the world than me, Lord love you, and so much for *that* elimination. You've got to be careful you don't eliminate too much in the process of eliminating. So Jubel Stark and the boys in the back room at the Warbonnet can't be eliminated just yet and what can you tell me about that Irish spitfire, Maureen Flannery, and her rough riders of the Rocking H?"

Katrinka said, "I can't tell you much. I've seen her at a distance, riding in with a herd to be shipped east by rail. I've never been introduced to her. I don't know many who have. She seems to think she's some sort of pagan princess, surrounded by retainers packing six-guns and not to be spoken to unless she summons you to come forth, kneel down, and beg for her clemency."

The big natural blonde added, murderously, "Even from across a street you can see she touches up her hair!"

"She's henna rinsed?" asked Longarm idly, only trying to picture the wildwoman he'd never yet seen, then feeling sort of foolish when the one more handy to him sniffed.

"Black as the India ink she probably dips it in and hanging halfway down her back. Rides astride like a man, wearing pants and a bolero jacket two sizes too tight for her overdevelopment. No white woman has natural hair that straight and black."

Longarm said, "Thanks for reminding me not to jump to conclusions some more. Regardless of what she looks like, Jubel Stark seems to have the Indian sign on her. Wasn't worried about the big Chicago Hardware outfit that salesman was working for when Chinks Potter shot his toe off. Yet a natural she-bear fired two of her cubs just for riding across the front yard of somebody Jubel Stark admires. So what might he have hanging over her? According to what I just read, earlier, she owns her own home spread and nobody owns the green grass growing all around. So she's never had to rent from Jubel Stark and if she's ever owed him money, how come she hasn't been able to pay him off, shipping well-grazed beef in considerable bulk?"

Katrinka confessed she didn't know and asked if he didn't feel sleepy yet. So he told her to let go and float off any time she had a mind to and then, once she had, he got up to fumble for his six-gun and a box of waterproof Mexican matches before he padded barefoot back to her office, lit the desk lamp, and started searching through the clippings in her morgue some more.

At the same time, in different places, Uncle Roy Sanderson's deputies had been searching high and low, lighting street lamps the laid-up Peg Leg Ferris couldn't manage lest they miss a tall dark stranger in the dark. So Deputy McBride sounded mighty sure of himself as he joined his superiors in the back room of the Warbonnet to flatly declare, "He ain't in Sioux Siding. I asked at both liveries and he never hired a mount to head north for the county seat, as some feared."

Judge Boswell, seated with Uncle Roy, Cherokee Adare and Jubel Stark at the card table, with no cards on the table, opined, "I never held I was *worried* about Longarm riding to the county seat. I said it would be a logical move. The county clerk up yonder has all the deeds to all the properties in this unincorporated village on file."

Cherokee asked, "What might be on file that anyone here needs to get all worry-warted over?"

The blacksmith turned to Jubel Stark to slyly ask, "You do hold legal title to that forge you hired out to me, don't you, Mr. Stark?"

The lean and hungry looking older man in a rusty black suit worn over immaculate white linen quietly replied, "Foreclosed on the blacksmith who was there before you, prim and proper, with all the proceedings on file with the county clerk and not one word misspelled. Are you by any chance starting up with me, you unwashed redskin?"

Cherokee gulped and hastily replied, "Hell no, Mr. Stark. Everybody knows better than to start up with *you*! I was just trying to be funny."

Jubel Stark stared thoughtfully at Cherokee, not a pretty sight, then decided, "I don't hear myself laughing. Get away from me. You bother me. I don't see why you were invited to this sit-down to begin with."

Cherokee grinned sheepishly and tried, "Aw, you don't really mean that, do you, Mr. Stark?"

Uncle Roy said, "He means it and you'd better do as he says, Cherokee. I hope I don't have to say that again."

So Cherokee got up and left. Cherokee was no fool. After he had, Uncle Roy said, "The breed meant no harm, Mister Stark. He just feels uneasy and talks too much around white men."

Jubel Stark murmured, "I just said that. Deputy

McBride, there, was trying to tell us where Longarm might be found."

The younger and thicker-set McBride said, "No I wasn't. I was telling you that tall drink of trouble must have caught that westbound varnish this afternoon, like Martinez said."

Uncle Roy soberly suggested, "Unless he went back to Widow Epworth's for some . . . home cooking. I'm minded of my first wife when I recall how we stood toe-to-toe with Longarm lying in my face, bold as brass, knowing I knew he knew I knew where he'd been while that Army cot was taking six bullets meant for his pesky ass!"

"He's too tricky by half," Judge Boswell opined, adding, "After you told me he'd bareface lied to me in this very room I went back over his sworn deposition, seeing it's a sin to tell a lie under oath, and even knowing what he'd been trying to hide, going over his exact words with a legal-toothed comb, I couldn't nail him with a single falsehood. For he never made one single false statement. He just neglected to mention he'd been damn close, if not exactly *where* all those guns were going off. So he knew both that buffalo rifle and that six-gun had been fired to clean his plow and he didn't want us to know he knew that. So how much do you reckon he knows?"

Uncle Roy said, "Nothing, yet, unless he likes to skate on thin ice indeed. Him and me are both sworn peace officers, required by statute law to share information leading to the possible arrest of a felon. He knows he'd be risking his badge if he held out on me serious."

Judge Boswell demured. "He lied to you about where he was when that army cot was shot to death, didn't he?"

Uncle Roy shrugged and said, "Could have been a white lie designed to protect a woman's good name. He wasn't lawfully bound to tell me who shot at him and missed, more than once, if he really didn't know. The question before the house is whether he's holed up with that half-breed widow even as we speak."

"He ain't," said Deputy Hernan Martinez from the doorway, having come in just in time to hear that exchange.

Martinez continued, "Just came from up yonder. Just pussy-footed up the back stairs and around all the upstairs rooms while Miss Magnolia served a late supper downstairs to Waco Walsh and Trevor Klein."

He grinned like a mean little kid and added, "Before I ducked out to toss the bedrooms I jawed some with those Rocking H riders and guess what, they've been scouting all around Sioux Siding for Longarm since they met up with him earlier today, rode home to tell their boss lady they'd failed to crawfish him out of here, and got sent back to settle his hash for him. Seems Miss Maureen wants to avoid the federal government charging her and her whole outfit for another dead deputy. So she gave Waco orders to do it discreet."

Uncle Roy raised a brow and snorted. "Waco Walsh thinks he's man enough to take on the one and original Longarm, even backed by that Klein kid?"

Martinez said, "I asked Waco about that. He was in a good mood, for him, and willing to talk, up to a point."

Martinez let that sink in before he confided, "Waco never came right out and said so, but reading between the lines I'd say the Rockin H has sent for some outside help."

Chapter 11

As things turned out, it was just as well they'd gone to bed so early and even managed to get some sleep. Because Katrinka woke Longarm early to declare that unless he meant to make his own breakfast he'd better screw her some more while they still had time.

As he did so, dog-style, the big blonde explained her paper was home delivered Sunday and Wednesday and so, since she'd put her paper to bed or had all the type bedded down in the galleys, she and her part-time crew of teenaged printer's devils ran the press downstairs a good lick of Saturday or Tuesday.

She assured him none of the kids working for her down below would know he was hiding out overhead. So he turned her on her broad but shapely back to finish right before he muttered, "Your town law says the Rocking H may be riding in before you're through downstairs. How much time do we have before those kids show up to print your paper?"

She said she'd told them to enjoy a good breakfast at home and be ready to start by nine, adding, "Our press run usually takes five or six hours. I treat them fair, even though they put in about the same hours as school kids. Could you move a little faster, dear?"

He could and for an all too short sweet time they were too busy to jaw about future plans. But once they were and Katrinka allowed she'd better get up and scramble some eggs, Longarm asked if she minded being saddled with a few other chores that morning, adding, "You don't have to do 'em all at once and any old time will do."

She said she'd be proud to do anyting for him that didn't hurt as soon as she had her part-time printers humming. She added, "They know what has to be done and it's probably safe for me to slip in or out as they crank and feed the press. Come on back to the kitchen and tell me what you want me to do as I whip us up some breakfast."

As they both rolled out of bed, stark naked, she demurely went on with, "I don't understand why, but for some reason I have a real appetite this morning!"

He allowed he was hungry, too, and as he got the banked coals in her kitchen range going again he explained, "For openers, I'm only human and I don't have eyes in the back of my head. So I'd best wire my home office for some back-up. If my boss, Marshal Vail, heads the pals I want this way about the time your crew starts up down below I ought to be able to ask the imperious Maureen Flannery and her riders what they want of me of a Saturday night with the odds a mite less ridiculous."

It was Katrinka, Lord love her, who pointed out she'd have to get on down to the telegraph office no later than seven A.M. if he expected his own friends to get there before midnight.

So Longarm stoked the range with more coal, kissed her, and ducked into the office to compose a coded message while she fixed breakfast.

She read what he'd block lettered as they ate. She told

him his wire to her Uncle Billy made no sense to her. He explained it wasn't supposed to make sense to anybody else but Marshal Billy Vail.

Katrinka washed down some eggs with her swell strong coffee and asked if Western Union telegrams weren't supposed to be private. He made a wry face and replied, "They are, and Sioux Siding is run by a small tight clique that may or may not include most anyone running anything in it."

So she said, "Oh. Ours is not to reason why and I suppose I could have an uncle in Denver who's been feeling poorly. Is that all you want me to do this morning, dear?"

He said, "Nope. Second chore may take you longer but it can wait. By now riders who've yet to see me have had my sissy tweed suit described to them. I might be able to pussy-foot better in these parts if I change my outline some. Even in broad daylight, locals who feel they know me on sight at some distance might be thrown off by someone just as tall, dark and handsome dressed more cow from, say, across the street."

Katrinka laughed and said she'd fetch him wooly chaps and a bright red bandana from the Dexter Dry Goods over on Market Street.

He said, "I wish you wouldn't. I'd rather shoot for nondescript. If I mix my regular hat, boots and gun rig with denim jeans and a darker work shirt it might require a second look at less than fifty yards for even a sober rider to recognize me."

Katrinka declared him a genius and allowed she'd get the wire off as soon as she could get dressed, then shop for his new outfit later, after she had her crew at work downstairs.

Longarm declared her a genius, too, explaining, "Nobody canvassing for me has any call to expect to find me

97

printing a newspaper and in the unlikely event anyone *does* ask your crew if they've seen me—"

"They're local kids with reps for being truthful," their boss lady cut in, adding, "They'll be telling the truth when they say they don't have any idea who or where you are. For I'm not about to tell them you screwed me silly up here last night!"

They kissed some more but held the thought as Katrinka slipped into high buttons and a summer frock to get on down to the telegraph office by the tracks.

After she'd left, Longarm dressed at a more casual pace, lit a smoke, and ambled back through the bedroom to settle by the lace curtains and keep an eye on the street out front.

Sioux Siding had been awake since rooster crow, of course, and by now most of the locals with places to go had gotten there. None of the few passing by afoot or on horseback seemed to be searching for anything or anybody. He'd just smoked the cheroot down and snubbed it out in a copper ash tray on the windowsill when he spied good old Katrinka coming back from Western Union and Lord have mercy if she wasn't built mighty fine, even with her clothes on.

He rose to meet the buxom blonde at the head of the stairs. She kissed him and said she'd sent his wire without a hitch. Then she told him she'd seen Trevor Klein down by the Western Union but the Rocking H rider had walked past without looking at her, packing his saddle and possibles roll as if he meant to catch the eastbound 8:25. She added the boy had looked sort of unsettled about something.

Longarm studied his options a spell before he decided, "Only way to find out is to ask him. It means breaking cover. But there's a chance I may get away with it and no chance I'll be able to let it lay if I let him get away without questioning him."

She said, "Custis, he's wearing a gun and he's a Rocking H rider!"

Longarm kissed her some more, rustled up his own gun to put on along with his Stetson and then, leaving his frock coat behind, went down and out by the back way, following the alley running in line with D Street until it led him to the U.P. tracks.

"So far, so good." Longarm murmured as he found he'd made it far as the vicinity of the trackside water tower without meeting up with anybody.

As he regarded the open space between the big wooden tank perched atop its framework of massive timbers he spotted Waco Walsh's sidekick in the shadows of that dispatcher's shed, as if he, too, wasn't eager to meet up with anybody else that morning.

Longarm took a deep break, then he was striding across gravel and through trackside weeds, with his gun hand polite, but on guard, as the Rocking H rider hunkered near his grounded saddle spotted him and rose to full height, looking comfortable as that cabin boy on the burning deck in that morose poem.

"I don't want no trouble, Longarm!" the young waddie called out as Longarm called back without breaking stride, "It's nice to see we agree on some things, Mr. Klein. You fixing to catch that eastbound?"

Klein answered, "I am. I've never had so grand a job. I doubt I ever will. But this game is getting too rich for my blood. My poor but honest parents raised me as a cowboy, not a killer."

Longarm glanced back along the tracks and said, "Train won't be here for a spell. Tell me about it."

Klein sighed and replied, "Like I said, no outfit ever treated me half so fine. Miss Maureen pays generous,

Fifty and Found, and all the found out to the Rocking H is swell. Meat on the table every day but Friday and the canned fish is most often salmon."

Longarm whistled and demanded, "Maureen Flannery pays even a top hand fifty dollars a month? Most outfits pay a dollar a day and feed you on biscuits and gravy!"

Trevor Klein sort of sobbed. "Tell me a tale I've never heard! Miss Maureen's spread is the closest I can ever hope to come to the big rock candy mountains. Highest pay, best grub, and they work you like a white man. I was never asked to perform one chore I couldn't manage sitting tall in the saddle."

He stared off into space and added, "Until recent. You were there when Waco as much as pulled me into a gunfight with a federal lawman. I told him later not to never do that to me again."

"What did he say?" asked Longarm.

The homeward-bound cowhand hesitated, shrugged, and decided, "May as well. Seeing I wouldn't be boarding no eastbound train if I was up to a fuss with my Uncle Sam."

He took a deep breath and confided, "They've sent for a professional to clean your plow for a nominal fee. Waco never volunteered his name and I never asked. I told him Miss Maureen was out of her cotton-picking mind if she thought they could gun another federal deputy and get away with it! I told him Uncle Sam has an *army* to send against crazy ladies who get too silly to abide!"

Longarm nodded soberly and said, "My home office wouldn't need the Army. Do you know for a fact Maureen Flannery or her foreman were behind that killing of Deputy Pitcairn?"

Klein shook his head and said, "That ain't the sort of secret one is likely to confide to the hired help. But *somebody* sure shot that old boy and Waco was grinning like

100

a shit-eating dog when he allowed this bird from Omaha would fix you good for thinking you were so good."

Longarm modestly replied, "I always try to do my best. Might Waco have volunteered any contingency plan if his fair-haired boy from Omaha fails to perform as advertised?"

Trevor Klein asked what contingency meant.

When Longarm explained, "Second round in the shotgun."

The cowhand brightened and said, "Oh, Miss Maureen says she'll just have to do it all herself if Waco's plan don't pan out. Like I said, she's a crazy lady. So much as I've enjoyed working for her, up to now, I am packing it in as far as her Rocking H goes. Like I said, you and that other stranger they back-shot were riding for the U.S. of A.!"

Longarm dryly thanked Klein for describing him in the past tense and asked if he knew just how Maureen Flannery meant to do him in if a paid assassin failed her.

Klein said he didn't know and added, "Like I told Waco when I told him not to pester her about today's wages, I don't *want* to know. I've never seen it, but those who have say that when Miss Maureen loses her temper she just forks herself aboard a bronc and charges like that Light Brigade in the poem. She won't be riding in alone if she comes after you herself, of course. I'm the only one who's quit, so far. Like I said, she's pure pleasure to ride for, most of the time, and such fine jobs are few and far between!"

Longarm allowed he got the picture and then, since every minute out in the open was another minute out in the open, he shook with Trevor Klein, wished him luck, and made it to Katrinka's back door without locking eyes with anybody but an old man putting a bucket of coal clinkers out in the alley. Longarm doubted that counted after the old man smiled and allowed they might be in for a real scorcher by noon.

But as he entered the press room he saw six or eight infernal kids at work or in a state of total confusion. It was hard to tell when folks you didn't know were at chores you weren't familiar with.

Katrinka herself was on the far side of the press as he came in and when she spotted him in the crowd, Lord love her, she trilled for her crew's attention and proceeded to lecture them about ink smudges as Longarm just went back upstairs behind their backs.

He hung up his gun and Stetson with a wry chuckle, warning himself not to tell Katrinka what that magician gal had said about misdirection that time, as she was directing his old organ grinder into position. He knew that magician gal wouldn't care to hear about Katrinka's misdirections, either, and as the morning wore on the buxom blonde proved herself the worthy rival of your average magical gal.

For though he'd expected her to, Katrinka never came upstairs all the time her young squirts were milling about below. Along about ten, after things were going smoother, she told the kids she had some errands to tend over on Market Street and nobody seemed to care.

So she went over to the Dexter Dry Goods to buy with her own money the jeans and work shirt Longarm had mentioned, picking duds of the right size from memory. There was something to be said for measuring a man from head to foot with one's lips and of course she was used to measuring on paper more than most folks.

Once she'd made her purchases and had them wrapped in nondescript brown paper, Katrinka carried her modest load back to the press room and set it casually to one side as she and her young crew worked on into the early afternoon. Then, after she'd paid them off and dismissed them for the day, Katrinka locked up and carried the package uptairs, where the now sort of anxious Longarm had been pacing some.

He forgave her with a laugh when she was able to assure him not one of her crew had mentioned him or asked what might be in that package on the windowsill.

He said he couldn't wait to try on the new outfit. She pointed out not a soul was watching. So he unpacked the jeans and work shirt, told her they were just what he'd had in mind, and spread them across the bed to get undressed and try them on.

But he didn't get to try them on until later. For as he was undressing, Katrinka was undressing and the next thing he knew she had him on his bare back on the braided rug, with her on top, a high heel on either side of his bare hips, as she went up and down like a merry-go-round pony on a throbbing brass pole.

Chapter 12

The new duds fit swell. Once Longarm got to try them on that afternoon. He felt more comfortable in the lighter cloth as well. Katrinka fixed her hair, put on a fresh dress, and made him a sandwich before she went back down to unlock her front door and open for late afternoon chores. Her delivery boys picked up the papers they'd be delivering of a Sunday morn late on Saturday and tradesmen knocking off for the week were more likely to drop by to place an ad in her aptly named *Advertiser*.

She came up around sundown to fix supper and report. "Vince Boggs of the Morning Star Saloon was just by to place an ad and ask if I paid for news items."

Longarm said, "That reminds me. About that telegram and these duds you picked up for me."

She insisted, "We've already settled that. I'm not the sort of girl who takes money from a man she's made love to! Don't you want to hear what Vince reported about some talk in his saloon?"

"Always," Longarm assured her.

She said, "We settled on my running his ad gratis and he told me some riders off the Rocking H were drinking more than they should and talking louder than they must have known. Vince said they were talking about you. I never told Vince you were right above our heads, of course."

He replied, "Of course. Did your saloon owner mention what they had in mind for this child, this evening?"

She said, "It appears they'd been sent there to meet somebody coming in on one of the westbound night trains. Uncle Pete runs trains either way, most every hour of the live-long day."

Longarm had known why they called it the main line of the Union Pacific or Uncle Pete as it was locally described. He asked if the saloon owner had told her anything else about the reception committee bellied up to his bar. She replied, "Just that they seemed on the prod and edgy. Oh, Vince did say the plan, as one put it, was for them to meet and back the play of this Mr. Something they were there to meet while their boss and the rest of the boys drank for public record en masse at the Warbonnet three streets away. Vince said he didn't get the name but that one of the kids dragooned into meeting him and pointing you out seemed to feel this wasn't fair."

Longarm shrugged and said, "It isn't. It'll soon be dark enough outside for me to pass for nobody in particular at any distance. How do I find this Morning Star . . . Never mind, I remember passing it earlier. It's as close to the tracks as the Warbonnet but back down the tracks a piece."

Katrinka gasped. "Oh, me and my big mouth! What are you going to do?"

He said, "Depends on what's there once I get there, on tippy toe. If there's nobody waiting for anybody I'll know the killer they were sent to wait for is already in town. If I spy what looks like two worried kids waiting for somebody, I'll know his train hasn't come in yet. Either way,

105

I'll know more than I know now. So I'd best get a move on."

He did so, slipping out the back way and moving down that same alley with his .44-40 loaded six-in-the-wheel on his left hip at half-cock.

He moved all the way south to Uncle Pete's right-of-way to minimize his chances of bumping familiar noses in the gathering dusk while, far off to the east, an approaching train howled in the darkness like a lovesick and lonely prairie wolf.

Crunching his way three streets east of the Warbonnet's, he eased on north until he was across from the Morning Star Saloon on the east side of that street. The street was lightly traveled at just after suppertime, but the saloon trade would pick up before long. So, moving in while the moving in might be easier, Longarm made it to the plank walk in front of the saloon and risked a glance in through the clear top panes of its front window.

He could see at a glance that the two cowhands drinking alone at the bar were still alone. So he had no call to study further. He turned and legged it back to the tracks, just in time to meet that westbound from points east on back to Omaha.

As the train pulled into the siding, hissing and fussing to a stop, Longarm lit a cheroot with one booted foot in the weeds and the other planted casually on the sun-silvered open platform. He only saw one man get off. But they'd never said they were expecting more than one.

As the smaller more dapperly dressed stranger got his bearing, nodded to himself and headed Longarm's way with no baggage but the bulge of the shoulder rig under his frock coat, Longarm called out, "You're late. We expected you on that last train."

It worked. Having been told he'd be met at Sioux Siding and steered to a target one could hardly miss in a

106

store-bought suit of tobacco-tweed, the imported gun said, "Wanted to arrive after sundown. Want to leave as soon as possible."

Longarm said, "Say no more. This child is wise in the ways of Uncle Pete and he'll have you aboard an eastbound varnish due to stop here for water within the hour."

The dapper little gunman asked, "Ain't that cutting things a tad thin? Are you saying you can show me to my target and get me back to these tracks within the hour?"

Then he was staring down the barrel of the .44-40 in Longarm's bigger fist as what he'd taken for a confederate dryly replied, "I don't have to get you back to shit. I'm your target. I'd be Deputy U.S. Marshal Custis Long of the Denver District Court and who the hell might *you* be?"

The gunslick who'd felt so slick a few moments ago gulped and protested, "I see it all, now. It's a fucking setup! You and that two-faced Walsh were figuring to trap my ass and split some bounty money, right?"

Longarm didn't answer.

The man he'd never met before said, "It won't work. Ain't no outstanding bounty on me. I always get away clean and where the fuck is your *corpus delicti*, here in Sioux Siding, if you're so fucking smart?"

Longarm nodded soberly to reply, "When you're right you're right. As long as you don't kill me I have nothing on you in these parts. So here's how we're fixing to work things out, if you have the brains of a gnat."

The killer, whose professional name was Butchertown Bill, had at least the brains of a gnat. So by the time his eastbound rolled in to haul his murdersome ass back to Omaha they were almost on friendly terms after so much time comparing notes, like enemy pickets might during a lull in the fighting on their front.

By the time Butchertown Bill was on his way back to

Omaha, more pissed at Waco Walsh than at a surprisingly reasonable intended target, Longarm had a much clearer picture of where the other chess pawns were supposed to be set up that Saturday night.

So he went back to Katrinka's and asked her for another favor, digging out the damned cash in advance this time. Then he paced the floor for a million years as she strolled up to the Aurora Livery and hired him a saddle mount for the evening.

After she'd tethered the bay gelding in the alley out back, the buxom blonde naturally asked a second time where he thought he was going aboard a bronc at that hour of a Saturday night. He kissed her, and she had to be content with, "When the mountain wouldn't come to Mohammed, Mohammed had to go to the mountain."

Then he was riding north along the alley, staying in the shadows until they were well outside Sioux Siding before he cut over to the main wagon trace. Riding sneakily through fences and cabbage patches was no way to pass discreetly through the night.

He'd felt it best to play his cards close to his work shirt because now that Butchertown Bill was gone, he was the only one for miles who knew Waco had left his boss lady out at her home spread with only a few guards and an iron-bound alibi while Waco and the others had planned to start a distracting brawl in one part of Sioux Siding while Butchertown Bill was shown to the love nest Longarm was said to share with some half-breed gal up by the municipal corral.

Longarm was still working on how Waco had come up with that notion as he trotted the bay north, knowing nobody could recognize him at five paces with no moon that night.

The cloudless Wyoming sky was so filled with stars you could make out the horizon all around, but you had to take the other black blurs moving away in the dark on faith, as cows. He and the bay would have gotten lost for certain if Longarm hadn't memorized the road grid on the map Katrinka had naturally had on file in her morgue.

Butchertown Bill hadn't been able to say how many guns Waco might have left at Maureen Flannery's disposal. After pawing through old newspaper clippings until he'd really gotten to dislike her, Longarm knew Maureen Flannery had come by her thriving cattle operation the easy way. The hot-tempered bitch had inherited the herd, down Texas way, from a dying uncle. Or so the story went. Longarm tended to take such stories with a grain of salt.

For while some accepted the famous hostess of Jungle Bob down in New Mexico at face value, as the niece of that cattle baron and accused cow thief, Big John Chisum, others held the beautiful Miss Sally was the play pretty of a dirty old man who didn't want the neighbors to know how dirty the both of them were.

Having met up and broken bread with the crusty but hospitable cattle baron and his niece, ward or whatever the sweet little gal might be, Longarm was inclined to accept Sally Chisum as the daughter of Big John's kid brother, Jim. But as a lawman he could see how such stories got started. A heap of them were true. In spite of more recent revelations to the elders of the Latterday Saints, there were still whole towns of old-time Mormons living outside their own Utah territorial statutes within sight of the transcontinental tracks and who was about to report a little slap-and-tickle between father and daughter, brother and sister or for that matter brother and brother? The law only dealt with the tip of that iceberg. Somebody had to *report* such offenses before anyone could be arrested for private acts committed in privacy.

So for all anyone really knew, the notorious spitfire

ahead could be queer for other gals or gang banging her whole crew after a hard day's work in the saddle for her. Paying them way more than the going rate and feeding them meat with most every meal would likely strike Big John and others like him as mighty perverse.

Having scouted Indians after dark in his day, Longarm knew you could sort of see things better by starlight if you didn't look right at them.

He rode on about as far as he figured he ought to and when he swung his gaze to what might have been a white blur, and it vanished, he looked to one side, reined in, and dismounted to lead his livery mount over to the sign posted by a gate of whitewashed lodgepole pine.

Striking a match, he saw he'd come to the right place, even though the sign warned it was private property and that survivors would face prosecution.

He tethered the bay to the sign post, saying, "Don't go away. I hope to be back in a spell. If I ain't, some kindly passers-by ought to untie you and lead you back to town before you can die of thirst out here."

Then he rolled through the bars of the gate without bothering to open it and set all those tin-can alarms aclatter. He hadn't followed the wagon ruts through the shortgrass far when he saw dimly lit windows up ahead. A yard dog that seemed to think it was at least a grizzly bear came to meet him, growling deep in its throat until Longarm tossed it one of the chicken livers Katrinka had given him from her icebox, and after that they seemed to be pals. Albeit he had to feed the mutt most all he had before he'd made it to the rambling house unchallenged and risked a look-see through a window.

He couldn't see why he wanted to talk to four old boys playing cards with guns on, so he crabbed along until, after peeking into more than one empty room, he spied a

110

cameo-featured gal about thirty, combing her long black hair in just her shimmy shirt.

The shimmy shirt was black lace and matched her hair. Her long legs and right pretty feet were bare as she sat at a dressing table, scowling at the reflection in her mirror as if she were mad as hell at her ownself.

They'd told him she had a mean temper. But as he studied on his next moves he saw she didn't have any guns handy amid the creams or stink-pretties spread out in front of her.

She sure wasn't packing a gun in her fancy undewear.

He moved along until he came to a side door. When he tried the latch he found it locked. But that was one of the reasons he had so many special blades on his pocket-knife.

After silently picking the lock Longarm eased inside to put the knife away, draw his six-gun, and ease on down to the door of that sultry gal's room. He took a deep breath, and then tried the latch.

Her door was locked from the outside he discovered when he went to pick the lock and found a key in it.

Muttering, "What the hey . . . ?" Longarm softly turned the key until he felt but didn't hear the latch click open. Then there was nothing for it but to boldly go where no man or woman had invited him.

Maureen Flannery let out a little gasp and froze with her comb in her hair when she spied him standing there in her mirror.

He was holding his gun politely aimed but ready for anything that might happen next when he quietly but firmly declared he'd come to have a word with her about her hot temper.

Rising and turning to face him, comb still in hand, the raven-haired and mighty trim gal of medium height asked,

111

"Who are you? What are you talking about? Are you that hired gun Waco was talking about?"

Longarm replied, "Not hardly. Butchertown Bill sends his regrets but told me to tell you he can't come to the party, after all. How come you seem to be locked up in here, Miss Maureen?"

She blazed, "Because they locked me up in here, damn their eyes, and I don't care who you are if only you'll get me *out* of here?"

He frowned down at her and demanded, "Are you saying they've been holding you a prisoner on your own spread, Miss Maureen?"

She moved closer to grab him by the shirt front, sobbing. "This is no time for fucking *conversation*! I swear I'll fuck you, I'll suck you, I'll take it up my ass for you if only you'll get me *out* of here! But get me out of here *now*, before it's too late!"

Chapter 13

So he got her out of there. The way she was. When he asked if she didn't want to put some duds on first, Maureen Flannery told him she didn't have a thing to wear. They'd made her strip down to her shimmy and locked her in her room before riding into town to set up a distraction for Burtchertown Bill.

As he led the way out the back, leveled six-gun preceding them, it was a good thing that growling, massive yard dog was on tail-wagging terms with its barefoot owner. Longarm was down to his last two chicken livers.

As it tagged along, tail still wagging, Maureen explained in a whisper she called it Gruff and that she'd raised it from a pup. She said Gruff was part Saint Bernard and part pit bull. He was mildly surprised to hear Gruff was a she. When he asked how come they only had one yard dog she said Gruff had killed and eaten the other two.

Maureen made Gruff stop when she threatened to eat the livery mount waiting for them in the darkness near the gate. He swung himself into the saddle first, reached down with the reins in his off hand, and swung her up

behind him to ride postern, astride, holding him around
the waist and letting out a strangled sound between laughing and crying as they rode out first across open range,
trusting the night vision of critters as the bay loped across
the sea of grass by starlight, with Gruff trotting along to
one side.

Aware the poor little thing was wearing nothing under
her black lace shimmy, Longarm slowed to a walk as soon
they felt safer. She never said but he knew some gals felt
it right uncomfortable, or right exciting to ride at a lope
with their naked, wide-spread love-lips kissing the smooth
leather so hard with every stride. Some said that was why
young gals were inclined to pet and kiss horses more than
young boys were.

They seemed safe for the moment but he was in no
hurry to ride on in a naked lady before he figured out
where he aimed to deliver her. When he suggested the
town law she shook her head wildly and said Uncle Roy
and Waco Walsh were thick as thieves, so he asked her
to tell him more about herself and Waco Walsh.

As she did so he was reminded of that adage about jars
of olives and wagon loads of watermelons. For unless she
was lying like a rug, a lot of lies had been told in her
honor and her true story wasn't half as exciting as her
legend.

She had indeed inherited a modest Texas spread and a
good-sized herd from a Texas uncle of the Dutch persuasion. She had indeed been fond of the young ramrod she'd
inherited with the herd and a small crew. So when Comanche raiders had shot him in the process of running off
some of her stock she and her riders had indeed tracked
them down, shot it out with them and recovered her stock.
She said she just didn't know how all that bullshit about
either side taking scalps had started.

He said, "I rode in the war. Sometimes, in telling how

114

rough a skirmish was, mere words come out sort of flat, and you don't convey the feeling unless you spice 'em up some. What happened after you lost your first foreman down Texas way?"

She told him she'd promoted Waco Walsh as the logical choice from top hand to ramrod. He'd been the logical choice because of how he handled cows, cowhands and, if the truth be known, she now confessed, boss ladies.

She said, "He deferred to me with the courtly manners of some English butler and with the fawning respect of a colored bootblack in the Deep South, as long as we were down Texas way, where I had kith and kin."

He asked how come she and her outfit had wound up in Wyoming. Her answer made familiar sense. Starting with Captain Charlie Goodnight just after the war, heaps of Texican cattle folk had resettled on the greener North Range, closer to the railroads east and farther from the Indians the cavalry was still reconstructing.

As the morgue of the *Sioux Siding News and Advertiser* had already told Longarm, she and her new Rocking H brand had prospered and grown in those few recent years they'd been up this way.

She said she couldn't put her finger on just when her hitherto fawning ramrod had commenced to push his luck. Thinking back she'd missed the first danger signs when he'd fired or gotten most of her old cowhands to quit, replacing them with younger less respectful strangers. She called herself worse than a fool for letting Waco hire back those two she'd had to fire for scaring the Widow Eldridge. But things hadn't come to a head until Waco had hired a slick lawyer and greased palms, without her permission but with her money, when Chinks Potter shot that poor dude in the foot.

Longarm asked, "How come you didn't take him to the law over that? I hope you never signed over power of attorney to your insubordinate servant! That's what they call push help who commence to act like they're boss, insubordinate!"

She sighed. "I'm afraid I did, but that was before Waco showed his true colors. As the man around the house and seeing he was better at dealing with cattle and cattle buyers than me, I let him talk me into giving him the powers to sign for supplies, draw wages from the bank, and write bills of sale for the Rocking H stock he sold for me."

When Longarm didn't answer, she said, "I know what you're thinking and you're right. It's a wonder I'm still alive. Why do you suppose I'm still alive, Custis?"

Longarm said, "I'm working on that. Waco ain't the first employee who ever took it in his head to take over. It gets tougher to get away with unless you can show your boss, alive, as a sort of figurehead. You have been offering coffee and cake to passing riders, showing up at public gatherings and such of late, right?"

She said, "Until this very afternoon I was allowed to play the gracious hostess with one of Waco's young thugs aiding and abetting me. I haven't been in to Sioux Siding for months. Things didn't come to a head until this spring, when I ordered Chinks Potter to stop teasing the kitchen help and he said he didn't work for me."

Longarm said he'd noticed young Chinks had a fresh mouth.

The boss-lady Chinks had sassed said, "When I mentioned as much to Waco, he just laughed and said Chinks had a point. I slapped his face, and then he punched me in the nose and said not to ever try that again. I bled like a stuck pig and not a hand was raised to help me. That was when I knew how much trouble I was in."

Longarm studied how to word it before he asked in a brotherly tone if Waco or any of the others had . . . harmed her in any other way.

She said, "I was expecting to be raped when they stripped me down to this chemise this evening. But I fear I'm not to the taste of Mr. Waco Walsh. I've noticed he does seem to get along much better with boys."

When Longarm didn't answer she said, "It's true. They're all like that. If there is one thing a Texas belle is taught, growing up, it's how to have her way with natural men. So think of me what you will but I was *scared* when I flirted right out with some of Waco's younger hands and to tell the truth it feels sort of insulting when you allow a man to sort of catch you unexpected in your birthday suit and he just looks through you like you're a pane of glass!"

Longarm didn't argue. He'd been called a queer, himself, by she-male suspects who'd tried to get him to let them go in exchange for some slap-and-tickle.

They said that when those French rebels came to carry Madame du Barry to the guillotine that time, she'd hoisted her skirts and offered to gang bang the whole crew if only they'd let her live one more night. But they'd cut her head off anyhow and they couldn't have all been sissies.

He decided Waco's personal life was moot. Didn't matter whether a gent liked hims or hers best to a federal officer until such time as he broke a federal law. So the question before the house was whether the Denver District Court had jurisdiction in a Wyoming labor dispute. Waco Walsh and at least some of the riders who worked under him seemed to be total bastards, but, so far, they seemed to be *Wyoming's* total bastards.

He said, "Last I heard, Waco and the boys are in Sioux Siding, looking for me. Won't be long before they're looking for you, too. If the men Waco didn't post back yonder to make sure you stayed home tonight don't look in on you now and again, they weren't paying attention when Waco surely told them to. So, since you don't want

117

to report all this to old Uncle Roy, your best bet is the sheriff, up at the county seat."

She asked why, in that case, they were headed the other way.

He explained, "We'd never make it, riding double on a jaded mount as your treacherous cowhands swarm across the range after us like angy hornets. So I'm taking you to a safe hidey-hole where, with any luck, another pal will be able to rustle you up some modesty and we can wait out the arrival of two more pals of mine. They ought to be getting in sometime tonight."

He didn't go on to describe Deputies Smiley and Dutch. He didn't want to scare her. He said, "Ain't nobody going to stop three grown lawmen if they want to summon the sheriff by wire, put a little lady on a train or in sum make sure her person and property are safe."

She snuggled her head against the back of his shirt, hugging tighter, as she sighed and said, "It's just beginning to hit me, how safe I feel *already,* Custis. Who sent you to save me? How did Cousin Una know that first gent they hired to ride up here and save me never made it?"

To which Longarm could only reply, "Slow down and back up. Who and what might we be talking about, now, Miss Maureen?"

So she told him and now he had a federal case after all.

Maureen, from her end, and getting messages out with the help of her skullery maid, had written to kin in Texas, telling them of the fix she was in some weeks ago. Her cousin Una had written to the skullery maid in Spanish to say she and her man had retained the services of a former member of the Texas State Police called Ed. They hadn't told Maureen his last name or who he was riding for since the Texas State Police had been disbanded. So until that very moment she hadn't made the connection

118

between distorted accounts of some federal lawman shot in Sioux Siding earlier that week.

Once she had, she gasped. "Oh, my Lord! Waco must have been reading her mail and he must speak Spanish! For can't you see, now, who must have shot your fellow deputy in the back, and why Waco did it?"

He replied in a less certain tone, "Makes a heap of sense. But I've wound up in quicksand leaping to other obvious conclusions. So let's eat this apple a bite at a time. Your sensible accusation ought to satisfy any court that I have just cause to haul Waco Walsh in for a serious conversation about the late Deputy Pitcairn. Meanwhile, me and the boys will have the power to guard you with our lives as a potential federal witness."

She asked, "What about Waco trying to take over my whole outfit?"

He said, "You can take him to Wyoming Law if we can't pin the killing of Ed Pitcairn on him. I'm hoping we can. It's about time we closed that infernal case. My point is, either way, Waco won't have any hold over you as soon as we fit you out with some decent clothes and a good lawyer!"

She asked what else there could be to such a simple mystery, now that he had the means, motive and opportunity figured out.

He said, "We don't. Waco or one of his pals may or may not own a buffalo rifle, and preventing Pitcairn from coming to your rescue, for a nominal fee he didn't want us to know about, was motive enough for more than one bullet in old Ed's back. But after that we're still stuck with opportunity. Who could have done it, and who can prove he couldn't have been the one? I just hate it when you have a crook dead to rights and he can prove he was in church getting married at the time of the train robbery."

She seemed so let down he added, "After that, Waco

119

Walsh doesn't seem to be the only one in these parts with mysterious holds over other folks. It hardly seems my federal beeswax. But as long as I'm turning over wet rocks. I want to find out how that one big frog gets all the little frogs to jump when he tells them to and, after that, I want to know which way he's been telling them to jump!"

She said she couldn't say whether Jubel Stark had given any orders to Waco Walsh. But she'd heard Waco tell her Rocking H riders not to ever in this world ride roughshod over any property Stark might have interest in."

Longarm said, "Bullies avoid brushes with one another for the usual reasons wolves feel no call to fight when there are so many sheep in this world. So it could work either way."

Somewhere another yard dog bayed and he spotted light in more than one distant window. So as they passed through the farm belt he swung over to the wagon trace and when that turned into Market Street he followed the alleyways to rein in behind Katrinka's carriage house.

As the nigh naked Maureen mostly watched, Longarm led the livery mount in to meet Katrinka's buckboard team. He led the bay into an empty stall before he unsaddled it and relieved it of its bridle and bit. Then he pumped it some water while Maureen put some timothy hay in its manger.

As he led the barefoot and almost just plain bare Maureen across the backyard she asked him, again, where they were going.

He said, "I told you. Lady of the house is a friend of mine. Unless Waco knows this, you ought to be safe here until we can put things to right out at your spread."

He led the gal he hadn't been screwing toward the back door of the one he had. Katrinka had heard them out back.

So her door opened before they reached it and the big buxom blonde, holding a candlestick with all her own clothes on, said, "Custis! Whare have you been! I've been so . . . Evening, Miss Flannery."

Longarm said, "Douse that light and let us get Miss Maureen inside. I just saved her from captivity and she needs some clothes, now."

Katrinka said, "So I see. Come on in. We have company upstairs, Custis. They claim to be friends of yours. A tall, morose half-breed and a jolly short blond man whose eyes don't smile when the rest of his face does."

Longarm heaved a sigh of relief and said, "We are out of the woods, now, ladies. I asked good old Billy Vail to send Smiley and Dutch. So now the rascals who've been giving us so much trouble are in a whole lot of trouble of their own!"

As Longarm led Maureen toward the back stairs, Katrinka moved to shut the back door, saw who was growling at her on the back steps, and called out, "What else have you brought home with you, for land's sake?"

Longarm said, "Oh, that's Gruff. We're going to have to let her come on in unless we shoot her."

So Gruff followed them all upstairs and didn't eat anybody, seeing they all seemed friends of her owner.

Chapter 14

Smiley and Dutch were waiting for them at the head of the stairs. Smiley was a hatchet-faced and morose breed, part Pawnee, who had never smiled as long as Longarm had known him. Smiley was his family name on the white side.

Dutch was as American as most but they called him Dutch because it was so tough to remember, let alone pronounce, his Old Country name. In contrast to the tall lean Smiley, the stubby Dutch always seemed to be fixing to bust out laughing, even though, as Katrinka had noticed, his eyes of sun-faded denim seemed to watch the world all around with the warmth of a butcher's cat crouched by a mouse hole.

Billy Vail sent them out in the field as a pair because he felt that either one could get himself in trouble, alone, but while working together they almost added up to one Longarm.

The morose but way more stable Smiley could track like a bloodhound and add things up like a pawnbroker's accountant. But after that he was inclined to think thrice before going for his gun or, worse yet, ducking. But he had a calming influence on Dutch.

Dutch was a tad quicker on the draw than even Longarm, and when firing for record, shot a "possible" or perfect score with every bullet in the bull's-eye. After that he was inclined to slap leather first, shoot to kill, and ask questions afterward, sometimes before such hasty actions had been called for. But Dutch was a good old boy who smiled sincerely as long as he knew you.

So it was Dutch who grinned as they shook hands and asked Longarm if he knew there was a grizzly trailing him. Longarm introduced Gruff all around and Katrinka said she had a chicken in her icebox that had started to smell as if it was time to serve it or throw it out.

Gruff retreated under the table with the uncertain roaster and began to eat it, bones and all, as she decided to let all these new pals of her owner live.

Longarm, Smiley and Dutch shared coffee and compared notes at the same kitchen table while Katrinka hauled the half-naked Maureen up forward to see about making her socially acceptable in mixed company again.

It didn't take his backup from Denver long to agree Waco Walsh had a heap to answer for. Dutch was the one who consulted his pocketwatch and declared, "It's going on midnight, even as we speak. What time does this Warbonnet they all hang out in close for the night?"

Longarm said, "When there's nobody there to be served, like most trail town saloons, I reckon. Nobody riding with Waco knows about me putting old Butchertown Bill back aboard the eastbound. Unless that hired gun was lying, their plan was to wait until they heard his distant gunplay, then start a barroom brawl to draw attention and facilitate his getaway from the scene of my demise."

Smiley added, "By now they must be wondering. Maybe having second thoughts. Surely on the prod."

Dutch said, "Hot damn, let's go kill the bunch of 'em!"

Longarm warned, "Not unless we have to. Dead men tell no tales and there's still some loose ends."

Dutch snorted. "What loose ends? Miss Maureen's pushy ramrod decided he, not she, was boss. When she couldn't get any of Waco's new crew to help her she sent home to Texas for help. One of her kin knew Pitcairn of old as a carpetbagging state trooper before he came to work for us."

Smiley nodded and said, "I hate to say it, but Dutch is right. It's as plain as day. This Waco found out Miss Maureen had sent home for help. It don't matter whether that Spanish-speaking maid was two-faced or Waco was reading her mail. Soon as he knew somebody like Pitcairn would be coming he didn't need to know who Pitcairn was. He, or more likely somebody he staked out near the rail stop with a Big Fifty, only had to watch for any stranger getting off where strangers seldom do."

Longarm started to ask a dumb question, nodded, and decided, "Few cold-blooded killers on the prod would lose sleep over gunning the wrong man and they knew Pitcairn would be getting off here."

He rose to his feet, adding, "What the hey, let's go ask!"

So Smiley and Dutch rose as one to follow Longarm. When Gruff came out from under the table, licking her chops, Longarm said, "Stay!" and it seemed to work. But as they were going down the back stairs, Katrinka called after them to ask where they might be going at that hour.

So Longarm told *her* to stay, too, and led his backup out the back and up the alley to approach the Warbonnet Saloon from the north by way of another back alley.

By then it was after midnight and Chinks Potter, seated at a corner table with Waco and the one called Bunny was saying for what seemed the hundredth time, "What's taking that razzle dazzle from Omaha so long? I swear it's quiet as a tomb outside and we must be the only ones still up at this hour!"

Bunny said, "He's right. All the regulars that were in here earlier left hours ago!"

Waco snorted in disgust and sort of purred, "Nobody left because it was his bedtime. They left because, just as we planned, they could smell trouble in here."

"So when does all this trouble *start*?" asked Chinks, reaching for his beer schooner again.

Waco snapped, "Don't you dare! You've had enough for now. Butchertown Bill will open up on Longarm when he catches up with Longarm. If Longarm ain't shacked up with that squaw near our ponies in the municipal corral he'll be somewhere's else. But how big is Sioux Siding?"

Bunny said, "Big enough to play serious hide-and-seek. I mind how, back home, us kids played hide-and-seek pretty good on a single farm. Longarm ain't a kid with his choice between the woodshed and the hayloft. Must be over a hundred buildings within a quarter mile."

Waco shrugged and said, "I reckon you never went fishing when you were a kid. Once you've baited your hook and have it in the water it's dumb to have second thoughts just because you ain't had a bite, yet."

Chinks asked, "What if the fishpond's empty? That Sioux Siding deputy I talked to earlier said they thought Longarm left earlier this very day, aboard a westbound. Uncle Roy had them looking all afternoon and nobody they talked to owned up to seeing hide nor hair of him since that train hauled ass."

Waco said, "I know Longarm better by rep than Uncle Roy, then. After we had that brush with him, I sent me some wires up and down the Owlhoot Trail. It was the same old cell mate who advised me to send for Butchertown Bill that advised me I needed somebody that good going up against the one and original Longarm."

"How would an old cell mate in other parts know which train Longarm chose to ride on?"

Waco said, "He wouldn't. He warned me the one they call Longarm hangs on tighter than a bulldog and never lets go until he's cracked the case or convinced there's nobody left to arrest."

Since rank had its privileges, Waco sipped suds from his own schooner and added, "They say you have to get away clean or kill him, once he's on your case, and I ain't ready to leave these parts, yet."

The more thoughtful Bunny said, "That's another thing that's been on my mind, Waco. You told me when I signed on we'd all wind up in clover after that snippy Maureen who thinks she's so hot winds up under the same. So how come she's still alive and we're still here where we have to *worry* about gents like Longarm?"

Waco said, "Let me and Butchertown Bill worry about gents like Longarm. Maureen Flannery's still useful to me."

Chinks laughed dirty and asked, "How come? You out to change your luck, with an unusual entrance?"

Waco growled, "Watch your mouth, Greek Boy. I'll need the owner of record's signature on a mess of papers when we're ready to haul ass this fall."

Bunny asked, hopefully, "Then we have your word we're cashing in no later than this fall?"

Waco shrugged and said, "There may never be a better time. The price of beef is at an all time high this year after weathering that slump in the wake of the market crash of '73 and everybody will be expecting the Rocking H to sell off a heap of beef, come roundup time. I'm too slick by half to put her home spread on the market. So with any luck nobody will miss her—or us—until the spring thaw next year."

"What if she gets away before we can split the proceeds of her herd?" asked Bunny, adding, "She's tried to, more than once."

Waco said, "She won't try to bust out barefoot when she's expecting her prince to come rescue her. From the letters back and forth that Juanita showed me, she's yet to make the connection between that dead federal deputy and the Texas state trooper she's still waiting for. Seems our Deputy Pitcairn was working on his own under another name for whatever reason."

Bunny marveled, "My God! You *have* been going down on a woman, and a greaser woman at that!"

Waco smiled thinly and replied, "It was a dirty job, but somebody had to do it, and my point is that Maureen Flannery ain't going nowheres until we dig the hole for her out back."

As if on cue from a stage manager with a sardonic sense of humor, the sort of swishy kid Waco had hired more for his looks than his riding or roping tore in from the darkness outside to join the trio at the table and gasp, "She got away! Juanita just two-faced to her room to ask if there was anything la señorita needed before bedtime and your Irish pussy was just plain gone, along with her big old yard dog."

As Waco and the others rose from the table the kid who'd ridden in from the Rocking H went on, "That yard dog never barked as we were playing cards near the front door. Somebody both Miss Maureen and her pet she-bear must have known must have busted her out the back and by now they'll be halfway to the county seat!"

Waco said, "It'll take the sheriff a good three hours from the time she gets to him to posse up and make it down here to Sioux Siding. That'll give us our choice between a westbound Pullman train and and that eastbound highball combination."

"What about our ponies?" asked Chinks as Waco

dropped a silver cartwheel on the table, thought better of it, and put it away again with a rude remark about Mahoney's mother.

Waco said, "Fuck the ponies. Let the sheriff find them waiting for us and ask around for us. With any luck we'll be well on our way to the Nebraska line!"

"What if they wire along the tracks after us?" asked Bunny as all four of them turned for the door.

Waco snorted. "Were you fixing to stay aboard that long? Sheriff can't hope to get her before three in the morning if he's already on his way."

He raised his voice to the other eight riders along the bar and the two at another table to wave at the door and call out, *"Vamonos muchachos!* Cat's out of the bag and we'll talk about it on the train!"

Longarm, who'd been poised for some time in the dark archway leading to the back alley, figured he'd heard enough. So he stepped out into the lamplight, six-gun drawn, with the ominously armed and dangerous Smiley at his side.

Waco and Bunny slapped leather as Chinks grabbed for the pressed-tin ceiling, crying for his momma. So he got to be taken alive as Longarm nailed Waco just over the heart, three times, and Smiley gut-shot Bunny so that Bunny could writhe in the sawdust like a wiggle worm caught by the sun on a brick walk while Mahoney from behind the bar blew another two off their feet with his double-barreled Greener before they could make it to the bat-wing doors.

Then some who'd already made it out the door were running back inside as Deputy Dutch in the street out front blazed merrily away with both his Colt 74s. Four of them never made it back inside. One of the four Dutch had dropped was the swishy kid who'd run out first, screaming like a gal as he'd beelined from that corner table and out the door Longarm had ordered Dutch to stake out. So as the gun smoke cleared there were five survivors, all told, competing with each other, trying to touch that same pressed-tin ceiling.

From behind the bar, Mahoney called out, "Why did we just do that, Uncle Sam?"

Longarm called back, "You did good. This was the bunch that murdered Deputy Pitcairn and they were planning to murder Miss Maureen Flannery."

The local barkeep marveled, "How come? I thought these boys *rode* for that Irish spitfire!"

Longarm said, "Never judge a book by its gossip. She thought they were riding for her, too, until it was too late."

Uncle Roy Sanderson came boiling through the batwings with Dutch and four of his own part-time deputies in tow, demanding, "What's going on in here and, Jesus H. Christ, it looks like the last act of *Hamlet*! How come you shot all these boys, Uncle Sam?"

Longarm said, "Had to. All but these five quivering aspen tried to get away or put up a fight. It's a long story and I reckon the federal courts will have jurisdiction, one of the victims being a federal employee. Can we put these remaining pissants in your lock-up while we wait for word from Denver?"

Uncle Roy said he'd be pleased as punch to board the bastards for Uncle Sam. As his deputies cuffed the prisoners one of them protested he'd just gone to work for the Rocking H and had no idea what all of this was about.

Longarm smiled knowingly and replied, "You'd do better offering to turn state's evidence and throwing yourself on the mercy of the court. I want all five of you to study on that before we take you before the fair but firm Judge Dickerson of the Denver District Court. His Honor just can't abide a big fibber!"

As the still shaken prisoners were being led away, Deputy Smiley took Longarm to one side to murmur, "You told us earlier you weren't too sure about the local law. What if sometime between now and then Uncle Roy allows that bunch to somehow escape?"

Longarm smiled wolfishly and replied, "We'll be sure about Uncle Roy and we're still waiting on the undertaker to come for the only ones that really mattered."

Chapter 15

It was after one in the morning by the time things were tidied up in the Warbonnet. But Mahoney had seldom served a bigger crowd. For there was nothing like gunplay—a heap of gunplay—to get everybody out of bed and buzzing like hornets from a bashed-in nest.

So when Smiley speculated on how many spare rooms Katrinka might have back yonder above the *Sioux Siding News and Advertiser*, Longarm steered him and Dutch up Market Street to Magnolia Epworth's place.

As Longarm had hoped, Magnolia had come downstairs and opened her stand for business, seeing there was so much business around the municipal corral despite the hour.

They found Cherokee Adare behind the counter, helping Magnolia serve the hungry maws lined up for warmed-over grub and freshly made coffee.

As he made the introductions, all three breeds went sort of Cigar Store Indian in that thoughtful way strange breeds met up in mixed company. It was likely because they hesitated to ask one another's nations in front of pale faces but didn't want to act friendly with a possible enemy. It would doubtless gall a Pawnee considerably to discover he'd just shaken hands with a fucking Lakota. Albeit Pawnee and Cherokee were sort of kissing cousins while Osage weren't members of the Lakota Confederacy in spite of speaking the same lingo.

Since none of them brought the matter up, Longarm didn't either. He asked Magnolia if she could put his pals up for the night. She said they'd have to wait until she shut her stand again and added she wanted a word in private with *Eestahanska*.

Longarm had been afraid she might. He'd been hoping she wouldn't, in front of another breed. When she joined him on the walk, they strolled along well out of earshot before she demanded, "Where were you last night? Were you with another *weya*?"

"Which other woman did you have in mind?" he answered without having to lie.

She snapped, "How should I know? For a settlement this size, Sioux Siding is crawling with love-starved *wasichuweyan*! I thought you might have shacked up with that new nurse at the clinic, having heard what my cowboy customers say about her playing hard-to-get."

Longarm soberly replied, "You have my word I have yet to meet up with any nurse at any clinic and didn't you just say she was playing hard-to-get?"

Magnolia smiled up at him to demand, "Do I have to tell a *tatanka* like you what a *wichincha* really wants when she plays hard-to-get?"

She didn't. Longarm said, "Don't matter what a gal I've yet to meet might want. And if we're to be *tawitankota* I don't want to hear any more *tachesli* about me and other women."

Magnolia sheepishly replied, "I thought we had an understanding."

He said, "We do. You're a fine-looking woman and

132

I'm only human, just passing through. You knew that the other night, upstairs. You got no more of a hold on me, and I've got no more of a hold on you than steamships passing in the night with friendly toots. I'm sorry if that hurts your feelings, *wichinchala*, but that's the way it has to be."

She sighed and said, "*Ee me doo kecha*. Can we go upstairs and toot some more as soon as I can close up shop again?"

Longarm studied on that as he asked, "What about your, ah, counter assistant, Cherokee?"

She said, "I never asked him to help out. He pushed his way in. I'll send him packing, put your two friends to bed upstairs, and then you can slip into my room and . . . toot at me."

Longarm had to laugh. But even as he laughed he was weighing the ways of most maids with most men. With that other gal under her roof in tight quarters, the big blonde might not feel up to slap-and-tickle and wouldn't it be a bitch if he turned down a sure thing only to wind up sleeping on that sofa in Katrinka's parlor?

He knew that no matter what he decided, Katrinka and Magnolia didn't know about each other. So on the principle that a bird in the hand was worth jerking off on a sofa, he suggested they go on back and get rid of those late-night snackers, first.

They did, and Cherokee seemed put out when Magnolia sweetly thanked him for helping out and said she had to see to her overnight guests, now.

Cherokee said, "You go on and see to them now. I reckon I'll just stick around until you're free to . . . talk some more, Miss Magnolia."

She counted to three under her breath before she said, "I've been trying not to sound unkind, Mister Adare. But you are starting to really *won ne tooka*!"

133

"I don't talk Creek," said Cherokee, sullenly.

Magnolia snapped, "Neither do I, you Cherokee pest, and I was telling you politely in my mother's lingo that you're starting to get just plain tedious!"

She turned to Longarm to add, "Make him leave me alone, *Eestahanska!*"

Longarm muttered, "Aw, bird turds, it's nothing personal, Cherokee, but you see how it is."

Cherokee's eyes narrowed to slits as he replied in an almost friendly tone, "I see how it is."

Then he turned on one heel and faded away like a thief in the night.

As they helped Magnolia close the shutters of her stand Deputy Smiley quietly said, "You just made yourself a real Cherokee pal, Longarm. You have to spend time around us to catch the full meaning of such gentle talk."

Longarm said, "I've been around your kind. Mexicans can be like that, too. One of the first things they teach old boys like me, down along the border, is that you seldom have to worry about a Mex who's calling you *pendejo* at the top of his lungs. The ones most likely to knife you seem to do so taking deep, slow breaths. But Cherokee can't do much to all the men around here he's jealous of. She's been brushing him out of her hair quite a spell, I hear."

Smiley dryly asked, "What does it matter how he feels about *other* men? Have you been getting any of . . . Never mind. Forget I asked."

So Longarm did. That was one of the things he liked about Smiley. The ugly hatchet-faced rascal was polite.

So Magnolia showed the three of them to separate rooms upstairs and Longarm allowed he'd pay for all three. Neither Smiley nor Dutch made a fuss when she said she didn't have change for a double eagle on her and suggested he tag along to her "office."

Once he had, as he almost always had before, Longarm marveled at how swell it felt to stick your old organ grinder in where it knew the way but hadn't been for a spell.

He never said it, of course, as he enjoyed her belly to belly and ass aimed at the rafters, but he suspected many a happily married man hit the whorehouses while many a Turkish pasha with a favorite wife or so kept one of those harems just so he could enjoy the woman he liked best better.

For there was something about the contrary privates of mankind that made a man certain the gal next door had to be better in bed by the time that first moon of honey was winding down, even if it wasn't true. Old Professor Darwin's scandalous theory of evolution held that early man had evolved to screw every woman he could get at or, failing that, any sheep that would let him, but, after that, men and women who'd been at it a spell got to screwing better. So it was a poser and many a man had been shot by the husband of a woman who hadn't screwed half as good as his wife back home.

Thus, it felt exciting to explore new territory and grand to come in familiar surroundings, and when you shoved it into a gal you were used to moving with after taking it out of another gal the results were sort of bittersweet, sweet and sour or, as in this case, downright inspirational.

"How! Tawitan owihankeshni and what's got into you tonight?" she moaned as she wrapped her tawny legs around his waist and thrust in time with him.

Longarm savvied just enough of her Osage to wish she hadn't said she wanted to fuck him forever. But he only said he'd been saving up for that night and once they'd gotten around to dog-style again he got to picturing the big ivory rump of Katrinka superimposed on the tawny trimmer hips of Magnolia and wouldn't *that* be a night to remember if only things like that were possible?

After the two of them had come thrice they stopped by tacit agreement for a smoke and cuddle. It gave her the chance to ask him in a soft sad tone when he'd be saying *how ke che wa* forever.

He put the cheroot to her lips to shush her as he said, "Forever is a long time and Wyoming ain't that far from anywhere. Smiley and Dutch will be transporting those prisoners down to the federal house of detention in Denver, by way of Cheyenne, come morning. I still have some loose end to tie up here in Sioux Siding."

She passed the cheroot back and grabbed for his old organ grinder as she said, "*Wastey!* But I thought you said you killed or captured all the gang behind the death of Deputy Pitcairn, *Eestahanska*."

He said, "We have. Accoring to the one called Bunny, Waco Walsh was the one who ordered the killing and Chinks Potter pulled the trigger."

"Then what am I missing?" she asked.

He said, "Who conked Peg Leg Ferris over the head to shoot me in the dark the other night, for one thing. Who shot up that army cot just down the way for another. Old Bunny was singing like a canary by the time they led him away in handcuffs, and he swears nobody riding for the Rocking H could have done either deed."

She shuddered closer and said, "Brrr, that's sort of *wo-wakan* when you think of somebody *else* prowling around in the dark like a *wanagi*! But didn't you say he shot at you with a buffalo rifle, the same as the one that killed that other deputy?"

Longarm replied, "Last I heard, Sharps and Hawkins Arms made them Big Fifties by the carload. You can buy such antiques off most any pawnshop. The sneak playing in the dark with me hoped to make it look as if he, she, or it was the same rascal who gunned Pitcairn. When that didn't work, he, she, or it snuck in outside and up the steps to empty a wheel of pistol rounds into that cot I'd just vacated, and I still owe you for that."

She laughed and began to stroke his manhood as she purred, "I'll take it out in trade. Why, do you say he, she, or it?"

He explained, "I try not to picture a suspect until I know who I may be after. Since I've no idea of my would-be killer's *motive*, I have to say a man, a woman, or something in between."

"But I thought you and your friends rounded up all those riders off the Rocking H," she whispered, stroking smoothly.

He said, "So Bunny says. On the other hand he could just be telling us things he thinks we want to hear and whoever may be out to kill me ain't the only loose end by half."

Interested enough to stop what she was doing down yonder, Magnolia asked, "There's more?"

He said, "Yep. Ever since I got here, half the folks, including folks who should have been on my side, have acted spooked and unwilling. They tried to talk me into leaving before I was even warm. I suspect I know who gave such orders. I want to know why, and I want to know *how*. How does one old skinny soul get to boss half the people all of the time but half of the people none of the time?"

She said she didn't understand.

He said, "That makes two of us. Talking to you, you don't seem scared of Jubel Stark at all."

She laughed, began to stroke again and asked, "Why should I? He's never tried to push me around. I don't owe him anything. He's never asked anything of me. Not even a cup of coffee downstairs. I've heard he's rich. I see him around Sioux Siding every day or so. But he's not *wo-wakan*."

Longarm said, "Others have said the same. Others can't seem to. It seems you either jump when Jubel Stark yells Froggy or he never bothers you at all. Ain't that a bitch?"

He was still stewing about that as he remounted her to reward her for her manual dexterity. They'd gotten to that less excited stage midway between satisfying an urge and wondering what was so urgent. She was a good old gal and it still felt fine down yonder, but he was commencing to look forward to seeing if he could force Katrinka's bigger thighs as far apart.

Katrinka wasn't afraid of Jubel Stark, either. Nor did they seem all that interested in him at the Morning Star Saloon. Yet Uncle Roy seemed under his thumb and he just about held court in the back room of the Warbonnet.

"He has some hold on some of the folk hereabouts and knows better than to mess with those he hasn't."

"What are you talking about? I was *about* to come, you *heyoka*!"

So he treated her right and she forgave him with a whoop he suspected Smiley and Dutch must have heard if they were still on the premises.

But at breakfast the next morning neither said anything or grinned at him or Magnolia dirty. So he felt no call to explain Indian uprisings they might have heard. Albeit Dutch did stare down at his plate with a Mona Lisa expression when Longarm said he had to stay in Sioux Siding to tie up some loose ends while they transported the prisoners in chains.

Since neither asked, Longarm told them at least one shootist was left over and they seemed to find that a reasonable quest.

But when he got to how one got to be such a big frog

138

in a little puddle Smiley shook his head and said, "You will never come up with a solid answer as to why some men are bossy while others allow themselves to be bossed. You can see a Jubel Stark in the bud in any schoolyard. You don't have to look far to find men like Uncle Roy, missing the walrus mustache, but kissing up to budding Starks and bossing other kids in turn. You're talking human nature, not mystery, pard."

Longarm shrugged and replied, "Hope you're right. Have no jurisdiction over just plain bossy dispositions. Got to make sure the old skinflint is a natural bully within the law."

"What can you do if you *do* find he's holding something over Uncle Roy and the boys in that back room?" asked Smiley in a weary tone.

To which Longarm could only reply, "Make him stop, of course."

Chapter 16

Longarm called a halt along the way and bet one of the stable hands at the Aurora Livery four bits he couldn't find his way to that carriage house and get that bay back where it belonged.

Once he'd lost the bet he walked Smiley and Dutch down to the Sioux Siding lockup, where Uncle Roy had just fed the prisoners a breakfast of bread and beans, which was included in the room-and-board fee he meant to charge to Uncle Sam.

Dutch wanted to argue. Longarm told Uncle Roy where to send the bill, and when they lined the five prisoners up the three handcuff sets the three lawman had between them left one prisoner over. So Longarm asked Uncle Roy to bill the federal goverment for two more sets if he had them. Uncle Roy did. When Smiley pointed out they only needed four sets to string five prisoners together Longarm said, "I know. I may want to cuff somebody we ain't caught, yet."

Uncle Roy looked surprised, smiled uncertainly under his gray walrus mustache, and said, "I thought you gents were through, here. What Waco Walsh was trying to pull was bodacious, and I agree Chinks shooting that federal deputy in the back gives you jurisdiction. But, no offense, I am *law* in these parts and I'll thank you to deal me in on it if you are out to arrest anybody in *my* jurisdiction!"

Longarm soothed him. "I ain't ready to say there's any just cause for me to more than ask some questions about a few loose ends."

"What loose ends?" the older lawman demanded.

So there it was, awkward to explain as a shit streak on a pillowcase and Longarm silently cussed himself for the slip. But the older lawman who seemed to dance to Jubel Stark's tune would have asked once he saw only two federal men were leaving with the prisoners.

Nodding toward the prisoners, Longarm murmured, "Let's not talk about where the babies might come from in front of the children. I'll tell you later."

It worked. Uncle Roy didn't press the matter and Longarm hadn't told a bare-faced lie, when you studied on it. Albeit he was still faced with the question of how you told a fellow lawman he was under investigation if you expected to catch him farting in church?

You couldn't, of course, but the orders were iron-bound-specific on federal lawmen being required to pay courtesy calls, state their names and beeswax, and level with the local law.

Since he didn't have that bridge to cross just yet, Longarm helped Smiley and Dutch frog march the now mighty crestfallen Rocking H riders down to the siding and wait on the platform with them until a morning westbound combination paused for a drink and all but Longarm got aboard. Neither Uncle Roy nor any of his part-time half-ass local deputies had seen fit to see them off.

Longarm was glad. If the old walrus was sulking, or waiting on orders from anybody, nobody had to lie to him just yet. So Longarm legged it over to F Street, which was mostly residential, and headed north until he came to an imposing mansard-roofed and mustard-colored mansion with a good-sized and well-kept flower bed in the center of its summer-brown but neatly mowed lawn. Katrinka had told him what the Eldridge place would look like.

Sine he was still dressed more cowboy than the current federal dress code called for, Longarm got out his badge and pinned it to the front of his work shirt as he strode up the brick walk. A small neatly lettered sign posted near the front porch steps directed anyone looking for the clinic of Doctor Wordsworth Shaver G.P. around to a side entrance. Longarm went straight ahead to the front door and twisted the bell crank.

After a time the door opened and a gnome, or a mighty short butler in dark green livery, told him the Widow Eldridge was indisposed and not receiving gentleman callers.

To which Longarm replied, "I ain't no gentleman caller; I'm a deputy U.S. marshal and why don't we ask your boss lady how she feels about that?"

The gnome told him to wait, and he did. He was starting to get mighty pissed when the gnome finally opened up to declare Madame was willing to receive him if he'd walk this way.

Longarm's legs were too long to walk that way. He took off his Stetson and the dwarfish butler, majordomo or whatever showed him into a drawing room where a silver-haired but still handsome woman in, say, her seventies rose from her sofa seat to extend a hand and allow she was Miss Stella, the widow of the late Doc Eldridge.

Not sure whether he was expected to kiss her hand or shake it, Longarm brushed the back of it with his mustache and figured that had been the expected way to act when she sat him on the sofa beside her and told the gnome, Wilfred, they'd be having some tea.

142

As the gnome waddled off Stella Eldridge asked what else they might do for the U.S. of A., making him feel important. He said he wasn't quite sure and filled her in on recent events in Sioux Siding and out to the Rocking H. By the time he had her up to speed Wilfred was back with a tray almost as big as he was.

The gnome set the tea service and a platter of Napoleon pastries on the teakwood oriental-looking coffee table and offered to pour. But she allowed she'd take over and dismissed him.

As Wilfred left she poured and asked if he wanted cream and sugar. When he said he took his coffee black and his tea Chinese she nodded in approval and said, "Tell me more about that poor young Maureen Flannery. Is she all right? You didn't say where she's staying here in Sioux Siding."

Longarm said, "We've hid her out 'til we can get her a lawyer out of Cheyenne. Ain't certain how many deals Waco Walsh made in her name and whether she'll be able to get out of the debts he ran up or recover any money. After that we'll still want to secure her spread before she rides out to it again. By my own last tally there were at least three of Waco's pals out yonder. They may or may not have lit out by now. I know I would if I was in their fix. On the other hand, the jailhouses of this land are not in direct competition with Harvard University."

As she pressed a Napoleon that looked too pretty to bite into on him, the gracious older woman said, "I'm so pleased to hear I seem to have misjudged Maureen. I had some trouble with Rocking H riders a while back and although she discharged them and offered to pay damages, I later heard they'd been hired back. But I see, now, both of us were victimized by that same forward foreman."

Longarm nodded, washed down the almost too sweet morsel in his mouth with astringent green tea and confessed, "That's one of the things I'm here to ask about, Miss Stella. I understand you and your property, here, are sort of under the wing of Mister Jubel Stark?"

She nodded and said, "Lord love a true gentleman of the old school. I was so lost and bewildered when my husband died so unexpectedly. But his friend Jubel took command of the situation and told me to just try and pull myself together while he put everything to rights. This used to be *his* house, you know."

Longarm allowed he'd heard as much.

She said, "My husband had a modest life insurance policy but left me a mountain of debts. Don't ever practice medicine based on the patient's ability to pay if you mean to die rich. But Jubel said to let him worry about everything and after a time I stopped asking him how on earth he'd ever gotten us out of debt and rented the clinic around to the side for enough to pay the upkeep on this place and allow me a cook and butler."

She leaned closer and asked if he could keep a secret for a lady.

When he allowed he'd try she confided, "I've naturally gotten to know young Doctor Shaver since he began practicing medicine on the premises, and it didn't take me long to find out he's paying less than half as much rent into my account with Jubel's land management firm as Jubel said! When I confronted Jubel and declared I didn't want to be treated as a charity case he just laughed and said he'd owed my late husband more than he could ever repay for some medical treatments too delicate to go into."

She sighed and said, "I don't know whether he was telling me the truth or trying to lull my conscience with a gallant lie. I'm afraid I was in no position to argue."

Longarm didn't answer as he helped himself to another Napoleon.

She said, "I know what you're thinking. It wasn't like

144

that at all. Jubel Stark has always behaved as a perfect gentleman in his dealings with me, and in any case we're both too old for that sort of thing!"

Longarm nodded and lied, "I never suspected different, Miss Stella. I reckon, since he never told you, there's no way to study on that sort of delicate condition your late husband might have treated Mr. Stark for?"

She repressed a shudder and replied, "If there was, the Hippocratic oath forbids any physician, or a physician's widow, from revealing any secrets about any patient to anyone else, including the law, I fear."

Longarm had been afraid she was going to say that.

She added, "Even if I were willing, I couldn't, because I handed down all my late husband's case books to young Doctor Shaver. He's naturally treating many of the same local patients and needs their past records a lot more than I do."

Longarm nodded and changed the subject to her flower beds out front. He didn't give blue blazes about her flowers and he already knew they'd long since recovered from being ridden though at full gallop. He wanted her to forget his interest in Jubel Stark's medical history before he made his next move.

He let her run out of steam on how tough it was to raise pansies and sweet williams on the high plains of Wyoming, even with well water, before he asked in a desperately casual tone how one went about getting to that clinic attached to the layout. She said she'd have Wilfred show him the easy route but naturally asked what he wanted from Doc Shaver.

He told her, truthfully enough, he wanted to know if a local doctor would be sitting in on one the county coroner's inquest, explaining they'd wired from the county seat somebody had to tally and record all those dead bodies in and about the Warbonnet.

145

As Wilfred waddled back in response to her pull cord, Longarm told her, "County says they only need that barkeep as a witness and Uncle Roy as the local jurisdiction for a pro forma hearing, when they get around to it. They might or might not want a local doc to offer an educated opinion as to . . . whatever."

Then he followed Wilfred out into the hall before she could ask him why on earth they'd need a medical opinion establishing the cause of death of a suspect shot while resisting arrest.

The short, stumpy butler led him along the hall, around the back of the staircase, and opened an inside door to reveal the back way into the clinic, built into the side of the main house a couple of steps down. A honey-blonde in a starched linen uniform with the skirts cut Rainy Suzy style to expose trim ankles in white kid highbuttons turned from the tray of instruments she'd been cooking over a Bunsen burner with the puzzled look of a friendly pup. So Wilfred introduced Longarm and she said in that case it was all right for him to come in the back way.

Wilfred left Longarm on his own with her. As she led him on into a modest maze of examining rooms to see her boss she said her name was Verona and that it was just as well he'd used the back entrance from the house because the waiting room inside the side door was cluttered with patients at this hour, just after church services.

He'd forgotten it was the Sabbath, damn it. That meant lots of places he'd meant to canvas would be closed.

As she prattled on, the nurse reminded Longarm of Miss Bubbles, that other honey-blonde down at the Denver Federal Building. He told himself it hardly mattered whether Nurse Verona was as ready, willing and anxious. He was already stretching his luck in Sioux Siding.

When they caught up with young Doc Shaver he looked even younger than Longarm had expected. He was tapping on the knee of an older cuss of, say, thirty with a rubber hammer. The doc told Longarm he'd be with him in a minute and directed his ,nurse to run Longarm into an empty side room. So she did, leading him by the hand until they were alone in there. Then she said, "Take off your clothes and put on . . . Oh, silly me."

Doc Shaver joined them before things could get really silly. Longarm told him what he was after. Shaver shook his head stubbornly and said, "Miss Stella was correct. I can't even discuss the furnishings of any patient's private quarters. Any practicing physician is naturally bound to see and hear things of a possibly embarrassing nature. We're called upon at all hours to often attend sudden emergencies. Some of them may be of a personal nature indeed and way back in Ancient Greece it was seen that few people would trust a physician with family secrets unless they knew he was sworn to keep them, as if he were a member of the family."

Longarm didn't answer, seeing the stuffy young cuss was right, in the eyes of the law.

Shaver said, "If I *could* show you Eldridge's case books they're no longer complete. They were out of numerical order with four volumes missing when Miss Stella handed them over to me. But just what are you searching for? What does it matter whether Dr. Eldridge was treating Jubel Stark or anyone else for any medical condition?"

Longarm said, "I've heard tell *some* medical conditions can leave a body touched in the head."

The young sawbones snorted in disgust and said, "I can tell you without betraying any confidences that Jubel Stark is sane as you or me. Sane as *me* at any rate. I've naturally gone on treating many of the same patients, including Jubel Stark."

"And?" Longarm asked.

"And I've said all I have to say about any patient!" the

sawbones said, directing Nurse Verona to show Longarm out.

So she did, the same way he'd come in, and Longarm found himself alone in that cavernous silent hallway. But he didn't need any gnomes to show him the way to the front door.

As he headed for the door he saw the sliding doors of the drawing room were now closed. That seemed fair. They called such rooms drawing rooms because you could withdraw in them.

He strode on and got halfway past the sliding doors before he heard a muffled moan of she-male pleasure coming from the other side of the oak panels. So he broke stride to give a listen, as anyone else would have.

He recognized the voice of the silver-haired widow Eldridge as she let out a muffled war whoop and sobbed. "Oh, yes, Wilfred! Yes, yes, yes and don't you ever stop at a time like this!"

Longarm sighed under his breath and eased on by. As he slipped out the front door with a weary shake of his head he could see he was right back where he'd started. For how could he trust the word of a lady of quality who fucked her own hired help?

Chapter 17

Like doctors, preachers and undertakers, lawmen often worked harder on the Sabbath than some other days of the week. So Longarm was surprised when he got back to the lockup to find it locked up for the day.

He tried the Warbonnet Saloon where, sure enough, Mahoney said Uncle Roy was in the back room with the boys. But when Longarm tried to join them, a Deputy McBride told him it was a private meeting and he couldn't come in.

So after Longarm had backed the Wyoming lawman inside with the muzzle of his .44-40 lending urgency to McBride's backpedaling, he found Uncle Roy seated at that table with Judge Boswell, Jubel Stark and four other stuffily dressed older men Longarm hadn't met before.

When Uncle Roy demanded to know why Longarm was trying to pick McBride's nose with a six-gun Longarm said, "Like the big bad wolf said, I aimed to come in. Wanted to talk to you about securing Miss Maureen Flannery's home spread so she can go home."

Uncle Roy said, "Ain't had the time, yet. We were just now discussing the funeral arrangement for Peg Leg Ferris."

"The old lamp lighter died?" Longarm blinked.

The local lawman nodded and said, "Doc said things go that way sometimes with a concussion. Poor old cuss was hit on the head pretty hard."

Longarm asked if they were talking about Doc Shaver.

Jubel Stark said, "Doctor Heflin, closer to the Ferris house. Why might you have asked about young Shaver?"

Longarm truthfully replied, "Just came from there. Didn't know you had another sawbones."

Stark said, "We have three here in Sioux Siding. What did you want with *my* doctor?"

"Is he your doctor?" Longarm answered innocently, adding, "Well it sure is a small world. I was up yonder asking about them Rocking H riders you asked Miss Maureen to fire that time."

Stark pursed his lips and said, "That's ancient history and I understand you and your fellow federal men wiped out that bunch last night."

Longarm said, "All but the three I saw out yonder. There were four to start but one rode in with news of Miss Maureen's rescue before he ran out the saloon doors to his death."

Turning back to Uncle Roy he added, "Never mind. I'll see about it my ownself. Got other chores here in Sioux Siding that press me harder, so I'd best get cracking."

Uncle Roy half rose from the table, saying, "Hold on. I don't much like the way you take the bit in your teeth and leave me and my boys behind in your dust, Uncle Sam!"

Longarm shrugged and replied, as he holstered his sidearm and turned for the door, "That's your misfortune and none of my own. Ain't got time to wait up for discouraging foot draggers to keep up with me."

Then he left without taking what Uncle Roy called after him personally.

He legged it on over to the Western Union to send another progress report addressed to Billy Vail's home address and, come Monday, sticking old Henry with some paper tracking. Like the crusty deskbound marshal they both worked for, Henry seemed to enjoy tracking crooks along paper trails sitting down, and the both of them were damned good at it.

It took a spell to block letter that many telegram forms. By the time he was lighting up out in front, the barn-red Lutheran church with a green copper spire was tolling ten A.M. As he shook out the match he spied a one-horse buggy headed his way with a familiar figure in white linen holding the reins. Nurse Verona waved and Doc Shaver nodded at him as they passed. He followed them with his gaze and saw they were headed for Uncle Pete's siding.

It was none of his beeswax where folks drove in their own buggy on their own time. He headed up Market Street, meaning to swing over to Katrinka's a couple of corners up. But then Nurse Verona came back up Market to rein in beside him and ask if he needed a lift.

He said he surely did and climbed up into the seat the doc had just vacated at her side. As she clucked the chestnut mare forward Longarm asked where Doc Shaver had gone. She said he had business in Cheyenne. He'd shut down for the rest of the Sabbath and told her not to expect him back before Monday evening. She couldn't say why, for certain, but she feared he was angling for a hospital staff position over yonder. He'd spent more than one Sunday in Cheyenne recently. As they drove north she confided, "The hospital head he's been sucking up to takes the Sabbath off, being such a big shot, and his wife is way younger and alone in the house all Monday, if you know what I mean."

Longarm did, but he asked, "Why did you say you *feared* Doc Shaver getting up in the world?"

She asked, "What's to become of me if he lands a high and mighty staff position in Cheyenne and I'm left here with nobody to nurse for?"

He said, "You'll have to look for another job. It ain't all that unusual an experience and you're experienced as well as young and pretty, too."

She gasped and demanded, "Who told you I was experienced? I swear no mortal man in Sioux Siding can say he's had his wicked way with me and what might have happened back home in Iowa happened back in damnit Iowa!"

He soothed, "Wasn't talking about that kind of experience. I meant you were a trained nurse of handsome appearance. You could find a position for yourself on the staff of many a big city hospital."

She asked, "Do you really think so? I wish we had more time to talk about that. But where do you want me to drop you off?"

He said, "I got plenty of time to talk. It ain't even noon, yet. What say we put this horse and buggy away and talk about your future in a more comfortable position?"

So they drove on back to the Eldridge complex, put the horse and buggy in the carriage house out back and, one thing leading to another and the both of them being young and healthy, they wound up comfortable indeed in her quarters off the clinic, with her trying to stick her bare toes in his ears as he commenced to hit bottom with every stroke.

She laughed when a clock struck twelve outside as they were unwinding with their heads and shoulders propped against the pillows piled against the head rails of her brass bedstead. Longarm had noticed right off she was built a lot like the pneumatic Miss Bubble of similar habits and warm feelings down Denver way. She in turn had confided he was better than average in bed. He didn't want to hear how she knew. So he proceeded to fill her head with sugar-plum-fairy suggestions about making her way in London, Paris or Louisville.

He didn't think he was doing her dirty. She *would* need a new nursing job if Doc Shaver left her in the lurch. If the doc took her with him to Cheyenne a few daydreams along the way wouldn't hurt her. He wanted to work her into feeling even more used, abused and hence rebellious as he bragged on having pals on the staff of Denver General.

He never mentioned names and he knew he'd never want to tell that red-headed Nurse Zenobia about Nurse Verona. But while she seemed as fond of fornication as her opposite number at Denver General, Nurse Verona showed more evidence of brains when he delicately raised the mattter of those forbidden case book and she flared, "Is that why you just took such cruel advantage of me, you brute?"

He said, "I only followed you home because I wanted to fuck you. I thought, as long as *I* was here and as long as them case books I wanted a look at were here . . ."

She laughed dirty and cut in with, "You sneaky rascal! If I fetch you those old case books and rustle up some soup and sandwiches, can I count on your company all afternoon and through the night?"

He kissed her left tit and told her to skip the soup but make a lot of man-sized sandwiches with no infernal rabbit food. And reflected as she skampered out bare-ass that he'd had to endure tougher nights on the trail in the name of the law. And if this got him in trouble with both Katrinka and Magnolia, a man just had to do what a man had to do.

He'd be leaving Wyoming in any case, as soon as he figured out what he was doing there.

So before that church bell struck one he was enjoying ham and cheese on rye, sipping cider through a straw and pawing through the seven tomes left to posterity by the late Doc Eldridge.

The naked honey-blonde in bed with him said such case books were sold with ruled blank forms in sets of twelve. If Eldridge had filled twelve, somebody had lifted five. If he hadn't filled most of the set out and started on the last, those last five wouldn't be missing. Who'd have use for a medical case book with blank pages?

He had to try, but he wasn't surprised to discover there didn't seem to be much to work on in the seven left. Doc Eldridge had recorded his case in the order he treated patients, not in alphabetical order. So you had to dig some for familiar names amid a sea of tedious strangers and when you found somebody you knew they'd only been down with the usual aches and pains.

He found more than one entry for Jubel Stark in the mortal flesh. The big frog of Sioux Siding suffered from chronic malaria and had an old bullet wound in his right hip that flared up when the weather was fixing to change, but otherwise, according to Doc Eldridge, he seemed in mighty good shape for his age.

Longarm almost missed the question mark Doc Eldridge had written next to Stark's given age of sixty. When otherwise honest folks lie about their ages they generally shave a few years off. When a man who sawbones thought he might be younger said he was sixty he might be . . . what?

Try as he might, Longarm found no entries at all for Uncle Roy Sanderson, Judge Boswell and some other boys in the back room, albeit Kevin Mahoney seemed to be living with a kidney condition beyond the scope of modern medicine.

Doc Eldridge had expected to outlive Mahoney. That only went to show the sawbones didn't know everything, and there was no shame to a condition that wasn't catching.

Searching in vain for something more shameful, Longarm asked if he could see more recent records of young Doc Shaver.

She protested, "Oh, no, I couldn't, and why would you want to?"

He said, "These older records of the late Doc Eldridge ain't complete, on purpose. Somebody lifted records Doc Eldrige was keeping at the time he died. Speaking as a trained nurse, is it too late to find out whether he died of natural causes?"

She nodded soberly and replied, "Unless he was stabbed or shot hard enough to still show. I fear he's been in the ground too long for even a crack pathologist to detect any poison but salts of heavy metals. Of course, if somebody broke his neck . . ."

"His widow said it looked more natural. Let's put that on the back of the stove while I see what a new doc has recorded about gents who seem to be missing from their old doc's case books."

She said it was wrong, but she wanted to see, herself, and so this time Longarm went over Doc Shaver's case books with a trained nurse reading over his shoulder to explain a heap of terms and abbreviations. Knowing so many of the entries personally, she was able to help him read between some lines. For like most doctors making house calls, Doc Shaver felt called upon to note unhealthy situations whether they were family secrets or not.

For how was a doctor to ignore the distress of a senile elder who had to be changed like a baby, wasn't changed often enough, and lay there in his or her own shit as their bedsores festered?

How did you treat the inflamed privates of a six-year-old somebody way bigger had surely been fucking, or account for an olive jar that had to be removed from an old maid's cunt by surgery?

Young gals living with rich old men were listed dryly as "nieces of" or more revealing "wards of" and if one big happy family surely seemed to keep all their slap-and-tickle within the family, how else was the family doctor to record young gals, with nobody calling on them, in a family way or dosed with the clap?

A sawbones worth his salt had to record and keep in mind how often, if ever, folks changed their bed linens or underwear. Young Doc Shaver had delicately worded how a railroad worker and his kin from somewhere on the steppes of Russia sewed themselves into their underwear in the fall and never came out for a bath until spring. Folks with other queer habits could come down with queer medical conditions. A doc recorded head lice that could spread. There were slatterly housewives who fed their families maggot-riddled leftovers resulting in awesome cases of mass indigestion that had to be accounted for, while home-canning could result in mass death when it was evident they were trying to preserve produce under untidy conditions at too low a temperature.

Longarm was amused to find a recent entry about a young lady of quality who bathed nigh every other day and changed her underwear once a week, and suffered constant backaches and trouble breathing before Doc Shaver managed to convince her she was lacing her corsets too tight.

He doubted the male patient coming in with sores on his pecker from jerking off too often with dirty hands would want anyone but his doc to know about that, and the butcher with boils he wouldn't stop picking at was not a butcher Longarm would want to have slicing *his* ham.

In sum, the very fact that few such intimate secrets had come down with the case books of the late Doc Eldridge meant somebody had lifted volumes of such juicy local lore, and as he told Nurse Verona, she could put everything back the way they'd been, he muttered, "Blackmail, pure and simple."

Then Nurse Verona was back, demanding he live up to the bargain they'd made and while his old organ grinder was more than up to starting over, it was early afternoon for gawd's sake and he'd agreed to fuck her until Monday morning!

He might have managed. They would never know. For they'd just agreed to catch forty winks when there came a tapping on the curtained window and a male voice was shouting, "Verona, you in there? How come you don't come to the side door, sweetheart?"

She gasped. "Oh, my God, it's Ralph! You'll have to go now! Get dressed and get the fuck out of here while I try to stall him!"

Then she called out louder in a sleepy tone, "You caught me fast asleep, darling. Go 'round to the door and give me half a minute."

So Ralph did, whoever in blue blazes Ralph was, and as Nurse Verona let him in, Longarm was up in the main hall of the Eldridge mansion, buttoning his shirt as he strode toward the front door.

The silver-haired Miss Stella let out a startled gasp when they almost bumped noses near the foot of her stairs. Then she said, "Oh, it's you. For a moment you gave me a start! I hadn't known you were in the clinic. I hope you were able to find something useful out?"

To which he could only reply, "I surely have, Miss Stella. I've managed to establish that a lot of things in these parts ain't exactly as things are supposed to look."

Chapter 18

It was just as well Sioux Siding wasn't too spread out yet. As it was, he had to do some legwork before he was ready to send more wires.

He struck out at the Baptist and Methodist congregations, but made a base hit at that copper-spired Lutheran church near the Western Union. The Reverend Horst Zimmermann had the time to spare between noonday and vesper sevices. So he received Longarm graciously in his manse next door and his motherly wife, every kid's ideal of a grandmother, served them coffee and cake while they sat and jawed.

The minister looked more like a kindly old uncle than an ideal grandfather. As he looked over the list Longarm had block lettered on a sheet of Doc Shaver's note paper, he said, "Jubel Stark, the land speculator, is a member of my flock in good standing. He's been very generous with his contributions and recently had his own crew repaint our siding, top to bottom. Wyoming weather is harder on exterior paint than we'd ever allowed for." He handed the list back as he added, "I fear none of these other names mean anything to me. Wouldn't your Mrs. Mahoney, Martinez and McBride be more apt to be R.C.?"

Longarm said, "None of the names on that list could rightly be called *mine*, Reverend. They seem to be dancing to another piper's tune, and I'm working on just who that may be and what hold he has over them."

The friendly minister allowed he didn't concern himself all that much with the worldly affairs of his flock. So Longarm asked if they could talk about everyone in Sioux Siding as long as they had the time.

The friendly reverend didn't see how any idle gossip he repeated could help, but the older man, who'd been there longer, verified a lot Longarm had already figured out and clarified some fuzzy details. As the minister went on about how things had changed since he'd built one of the first churches on the original and still mighty open railroad grant, Longarm was able to cut the folks thereabouts into three milling herds in his head.

The original railroading crowd strung out near the tracks tended to mill together. The earlier bunch who'd bought land off Uncle Pete while he was still selling cheap still seemed to run things and, now that Longarm had mentioned it, Reverend Horst agreed Jubel Stark was one of that bunch, if not the most important member.

He quickly added that neither Jubel Stark nor any other member of the insider crowd had ever abused any of the largest bunch of all, the disorganized majority who'd moved in a few at a time and didn't seem as interested in the running of things as long as things got run.

Jubel Stark himself, with his own money, had made many a civic improvement at no cost to anybody. They grumbled some about the property taxes collected by the distant sheriff's department, but nobody had any beef with Jubel Stark as far as his own minister had heard.

Longarm said, "That's an interesting point you raised about Mahoney, Martinez and McBride being likely papists. Am I correct in picturing your own flock as largely High Dutch, like Martin Luther, himself?"

Zimmermann chuckled and replied, "The Reverend Martin has been in his grave for well over three hundred years and his message has gotten around. My wife and I are, as you've guessed, of Prussian birth, and a good many of my flock are first- or second-generation Deutsch. But as many more, if not the majority, have names of British origin."

Longarm nodded but said, "I have found in my travels how many an owlhoot rider tends to steer his given name down another track. Arrested this old French Canuck who'd changed his name from Cartier to just plain Carter. The last white man to see Custer alive, Trooper Martin, was really an Italian gent who'd started out Martini, if you follow my drift."

The sky pilot said, "I do. Zimmermann would anglicize as *Carpenter* if we we were worried about that sort of thing."

Longarm allowed Zimmermann sounded all right to him, asked some more such questions and politely refused second helpings, explaining he had some other chores, however good their High Dutch cake was.

He went next to the Western Union to ask if they had any answer to the wire to Maureen Flannery's Cheyenne law firm. They didn't. Longarm didn't get his bowels in an uproar. It stood to reason nobody had read Maureen's wired cry for help on the sabbath.

That was why he wired Billy Vail again at his private residence on Sherman Street. He knew old Billy, the same as himself, was never all the way off duty if there were duties that needed doing.

Uncle Roy Sanderson was waiting for him on the walk out front. The older lawman didn't mince words. He demanded, "How come you didn't level this morning with them other federal men and your federal prisoners? Who or what are you still after here in Sioux Siding? You're supposed to *tell* me, damn your eyes!"

Longarm replied in an easier tone, "Like to leave a campsite tidy and make sure the fire's out before I move on. Have you sent anybody out to the Rocking H to make sure it's safe for Miss Maureen to head on home?"

Uncle Roy looked away and muttered, "Place will still be there tomorrow. I can't hardly ask an unpaid deputy to ride that far on the sabbath, can I?"

Longarm said, "I would, if I was the law in these parts. It's only a two-hour ride if you know how to stay on at a trot, and how come Sioux Siding doesn't pay its modest constabulary enough to do their jobs?"

Uncle Roy said the ad hoc town council didn't have powers to tax and had to pass the hat, adding, "We don't need much in the way of law, most of the time."

Longarm said he had to get it on up the road and Uncle Roy felt no call to tag along with a stranger who asked such sassy questions.

Back at the *Sioux Siding News and Advertiser* Longarm found Katrinka and Maureen in the pressroom, along with the massive mutt, Gruff, who thumped her tail on the flooring at the sight of a pal who was sometimes good for a chicken liver.

Both gals were wearing those printer's smocks, cut to measure of the big blonde. So Maureen looked sort of like a little girl playing grown-up in a tent, save for the way she filled out the smock around her chest. Katrinka had been teaching the young cattlewoman how to stick type and they were getting on like school chums.

When Longarm asked the newspaper gal if she had a county survey map on hand, Katrinka said she had one posted for her delivery boys in the storage shed out back. Then she naturally asked how come.

Longarm said, "Can't seem to interest the local law in securing the Rocking H for Miss Maureen, here. Uncle Roy must not want to wire the county seat more than he has to. I figured I'd ride out this afternoon and do it my ownself."

Katrinka said, "It's going on three. You'll never make it back in time for supper, and I just had fresh chickens delivered."

He said he'd try and get back by sundown. She warned him, "See that you do unless you want us to start without you!"

He went out the back door, ambled over to the shingled shed built as a lean-to against the bigger carriage house to duck inside, where, sure enough, a big survey map of the whole county and then some was pinned to the far wall. So he circled the piles of baled newspapers for a look-see, nodded to himself, and went out and back to the alley to stride up to the livery stable again.

When he got there he found the older gent who owned it working shorthanded, alone, because he was too cheap to pay overtime on the sabbath. Longarm said he'd saddle and bridle if the owner would pick him a good trotter, explaining he had some ground to cover.

The older man said, "Come on back and I'll show you what we got, only leave that pet bear outside lest it spook the riding stock, hear?"

Longarm turned to see Gruff had followed him from Katrinka's. He had to laugh, and when he said, "Stay!" the big Saint Bernard–pitbull sat her big shaggy ass in the dust to sort of grin at him with her tongue hanging out.

As they headed back between the stalls, the owner explained all *those* horses' asses belonged to private stock they kept handy for their owners. Not having stalls enough to go around, they kept all they had for hire in the corral out back. So once they got there, Longarm had to rope the frisky-looking paint he'd picked and fight her over to the gate himself. Albeit the owner did hold the paint as Longarm fought its head into the hired bridle and kneed it good to make it let out its deliberate puff as he cinched the saddle. You called the paint an it because it was a gelding. As he forked aboard, Longarm had to wonder what it would have been to ride with its balls still attached. When he reined it for the street out front it crow-hopped halfway there, spotted Gruff out front, and decided it wasn't going no place until Longarm whipped it good with the ends of the reins.

That worked, and by the time they'd circled the municipal corral on the side away from Magnolia's place with Gruff trotting after, the paint had settled down to an uncomfortable but mile-eating pace.

It sure beat all how different he'd pictured the scenery to either side in the dark the last time, albeit none of the pigs and chicken operations they passed at first looked astonishing.

Once they made it out to open range he saw more grazing cattle than he'd pictured by starlight. Neither the paint nor the yard dog of a beef spread had to be told how the barbwire fences starting to sprout across the Northern High Plains were meant to keep cattle *in*. Between roundups, the mixed stock of different brands was left free to roam the sea of grass as it chose, with home spreads, homestead, and growing crops fenced in to keep all those abling cows out where they belonged.

As he'd promised Katrinka and chided Uncle Roy, it wasn't all that long a ride out to the Rocking H. They made the eight or ten miles in way less than two hours. But he'd studied that survey map with the uncertain reception awaiting unexpected visitors riding through the front gate. So when he came to Maureen's turn-off Longarm kept riding up the wagon trace toward the far-off county seat.

Old Gruff, knowing where she was, turned to trot a ways toward her home spread, shot Longarm and the paint a puzzled look over her shaggy shoulder, and galloped across the tawny short-grass after them.

The method in Longarm's madness lay in the contour lines on that survey map back at Katrinka's. He'd seen right off how Maureen's home spread had naturally been claimed and laid out on the same swamping stretch of higher prairie the railroad survey teams had picked for their uncle Pete's main line and the siding Sioux Siding had grown up along. But according to the county survey, the high ground dropped off just past the Rocking H to drain east when it was raining. Most of the time, that afternoon being one of them, the lower grassland to the north was just a tad richer and hence more infested with cows.

Longarm rode down among them and cut west to follow the slope on over to Maureen's place. Anybody watching that approach would find it impossible to see a horse and rider moving below their skyline and the grass along the slope kept their dust moderate.

When he figured by dead reckoning they were getting warm he reined in, dismounted, tethered the paint to a clump of soapweed with roots halfway down to China, and crawled the last few yards through the grass on his belly to see, when he took off his hat and risked a bareheaded peek, how he'd lined up tolerably good, with an easy shot at the backyard, where a Mexican kid of around twelve was cultivating the small kitchen garden with a hoe.

Maureen had told him her household help seemed loyal to her. Longarm took a chance on that and whistled. When the kid looked up, Longarm waved him over. The kid approached uncertainly with the hoe held at port arms to where he could see what he was approaching. He stopped where he was and called out, "For why are you lying down in the grass, *señor*?"

Longarm identified himself as an *amigo* of *la patróna* and asked if the *ladrónes* who'd been holding her captive were still inside.

The kid laughed and said, *"Pero no, señor*, they left before dawn, along with one of the *chicas*. The rest of us suspect she might have been in with those *marisosos chingado*!"

So once he'd had a look around inside and agreed with the faithful household help about fucking butterflies Longarm strode back to the drop off and down to where Gruff seemed to be keeping the livery paint company. When he untethered the gelding and remounted, Gruff tagged along after them, even when Longarm pointed back the other way and snorted. "Your own bedding and likely your favorite bones are back yonder, you big mutt."

But when she followed anyway he reflected on the table scraps being as good or better back at Katrinka's. So he didn't argue as he tried to make it back by sundown.

He almost did, having spent no more than five hours in the saddle if you counted time on foot out to the Rocking H. The sun had just dropped behind the Front Range way off to the west, and there was still enough light to see colors as they circled the municipal corral some more. There would have been a brighter gloaming if the Wyoming sky hadn't been cloudless at that time of High Summer. Far across the city block of corral he made out the lamplight of Magnolia's food stand. With any luck she'd find it tough to tell one rider from another at that range.

He reined in and called out when they reached the gaping doorway of the Aurora Livery. There came no answer as Longarm dismounted and led the paint inside. As he did so one of the boarded ponies whinnied in surprise, and Longarm, remembering what the owner had said about spooking the stock in the stalls to either side, side-stepped to lead the paint back out and around to the corral the way they'd last left it.

So that was the second time he threw a tolerable marksman with a single-shot Big Fifty off with an unexpected last-second move.

As the buffalo rifle roared down at him from the hay-loft at the far end of the livery stable all hell broke loose as ponies stalled the length of the livery all commenced to kick and struggle to bust out. A dapple gray in the stall Longarm ducked into tried to kick the stuffings out of him but couldn't manage in the confined space.

The paint Longarm had been leading was long gone out the front. Longarm arm swung the stall door open and whipped the already hysterical gray with his hat to fill the walkway down the center of the stable with more confusion before he ducked across the stable to set a roan stud free as, somewhere farther along, somebody opened up with a six-gun, firing blind and hitting yet another excited pony, judging from the excitment.

But Longarm had made it the width of two stalls deeper into the gloomy depths of the stable and when he heard the metallic click of a steel hammer coming down on a spent brass he risked a run past the ladder leading up to the hayloft, hoping the son of a bitch would reload instead of going for a second six-gun.

As he made it into the nigh total darkness beyond, Longarm tripped over something too soft to be a log just lying there. He hunkered down to feel the side of the livery owner's neck, swore, and called out, "All right you back-shooting puddle of puke! I know where you are and we both know them planks you're standing on above me won't stop a round of .44-40. So what's it going to be?"

Chapter 19

It didn't work. For the same reasons Longarm didn't give his position away by firing up through the thin planking, the sneaky rascal who'd fired on him from up yonder didn't choose to fire down and, with all the riding stock snorting, stomping and whinnying in the dark all around, Longarm couldn't tell if anyone was moving about up yonder or, worse yet, still up yonder!

A voice out front called in, "I'm the law and who's in there doing what, gawd damn it?"

Longarm called back, "U.S. Deputy Long, here. Somebody's killed the old man who owns this place and just now tried to kill me! Cover the back way out! I got him boxed in the hayloft if there's no back exit!"

The other lawman shouted, even as he ran, "There's a backdoor and a ladder down the outside from the hayloft."

Then he was out of earshot and Longarm could only say, "Aw, shit!" as he muttered, "Ready or not, here I come!"

You charged down stairs or ladders and moved up 'em sneaky and slow. But when he risked his bare head as far down as his eyes, there seemed to be nothing up yonder but hay, and not enough of that to hide much. Longarm swore, climbed all the way up and moved back toward the open loading door outlined against the deep blue night sky. As he saw there was indeed another ladder leading down the outside of the board-and-batten siding he called out to his unseen backup. "Nothing up here. See anything down there?"

"Not hardly," came the response, "Come on down and we'll check out the corral and tack room together!"

So Longarm holstered his six-gun and swung out and around to climb down as he called, "Which of Uncle Roy's boys might you be?"

He was answered by a scream of pain and a fusillade of wild shots aimed his way but way to high. So he let go of the ladder and twisted in the air on the way down to land hard enough to haunch him as he got his own gun out and tried to make sense out of the dusty, swirling screams of agony and grizzlylike snarls until he made out, "Yeow! Jesus! I give! I give! Call this fucking wolverine off me!"

So by the time other voices were shouting through the night in the name of the law Longarm had old Gruff by the nape of her neck with a left boot planted on the killer's chest as he sounted, "Down, girl, down! That's enough and I thank you sincere!"

But by the time he had the Saint Bernard–pit bull off her victim the poor cuss she'd been trying to eat alive wasn't answering when he was spoken to.

Telling Gruff to "Sit!" and discovering to his amazement she obeyed, he thumbed a match head alight as he went on covering the cuss he was sort of standing on. It was Cherokee Adare. Gruff hadn't messed his face up too bad to recognize; she'd been tearing at his throat.

Some backup Longarm recognized as Deputy McBride in the flickering light came around the back of the stable to join him, asking the same expected questions as the match went out.

Longarm identified himself and struck another match as he said, "This mighty sneaky rascal knew I'd ridden out on one of those livery mounts, so he clobbered the owner the same as he clobbered Peg Leg Ferris the other evening and waited for me in the dark with that same buffalo rifle. When that didn't work he slipped down the back ladder, circled around to the front and pretended to be one of your boys. So like the fool I am, I asked him to check the back and he was waiting back here as I climbed down the ladder with my dumb ass turned to him!"

McBride struck a light of his own as he drew nearer, whistled softly and said, "Jesus, Mary and Joseph, I see that didn't work out as he planned it at all! What did you hit him with, a threshing machine?"

Longarm soberly replied, "Whoever coined the phrase about man's best friend had big old shaggy mutts like Miss Gruff, yonder, in mind. So don't make sudden moves around me. She seems to feel I need protecting. I never told her to sic Cherokee. I'd forgotten she was about. She recognized his true intent while I still thought we were on the same side. I expect the doc will decide she tore his jugular vein open before letting go. He wouldn't have been able to fuss so much if she'd ripped out his carotid artery."

Another voice called in from the street. McBride called back, "In here. It's over. Longarm just settled the hash of Cherokee Adare. Says Cherokee was the one who killed Peg Leg Ferris and, earlier this evening, poor Pop Walters, the owner, here."

The dapper Deputy Martinez joined them to gasp, "*Ay, chihuahua*! what did you do to him and for why was he after an old lamp lighter and the owner of this stable?"

Longarm replied, "I didn't do nothing to him. I didn't know we were at feud. He swatted two old men who were in his way like flies in order to shoot me in the back the same as Deputy Pitcairn was killed."

By this time McBride, who naturally knew his way around the local livery, had rustled up an oil lamp from just inside the back way out. As he shed more light on the subject, Cherokee Adare looked ever more sincerely dead, staring up from a great red puddle spread across the stableyard dust nigh as far as his overturned hat to the west of him and his double action Colt .45 to the south of him.

So when they were joined by Uncle Roy and a gaggle of others, including young Doc Shaver, already back from whatever he'd been up to in Cheyenne, he pronounced Cherokee dead. Uncle Roy wanted to know how come.

Longarm said, "It looks as if Cherokee here was playing a lone hand. We know Bunny Forbes back-shot Ed Pitcairn with another Big Fifty under orders from Waco Walsh. But Cherokee was vexed with *me*, personally, because he thought I had something he couldn't have."

"What was that?" asked their local law.

"Lets just call it popularity," Longarm replied, adding, "Jealous hearts and feeble minds can lead us into hasty temptation, and he figured he'd get away with laying the blame on already established killers."

He started to go on about the exact cause of Cherokee's death, took a deep thoughtful breath and said, "I guess you know this mess on top of my cracking the killing of Pitcairn is going to call for a full hearing before the county coroner, somewhere more formal than the back room at the Warbonnet Saloon?"

From where he'd been standing back in the gathering crowd, Jubel Stark in the flesh called out, "You let us worry about getting in touch with the county seat, Deputy Long."

Uncle Roy said, "Damned A!"

Stark went on, "I'm calling our Sioux Siding hearing at nine A.M. in the back room you seem to feel you're too grand for. We don't have a city hall down our way, yet. We'll naturally wire the county seat about this latest development and if they want to send somebody they'll send somebody."

"Ain't there supposed to be at least a deputy coroner present when we all get together in that back room?" asked Longarm mildly.

Jubel Stark didn't answer. He didn't have to. Uncle Roy said, "We don't need no big-city law clerks telling us how to do things in Wyoming, damn it. You heard the man say we'll notify the county about what we're doing. Then we'll damn well *do* it, in our own good time, and if the county wants to dispute our findings, let 'em do so in *their* own good time!"

Jubel Stark suggested in a jovial tone that anybody who wasn't fixing to help the undertaking crew clean up might like to have a drink on him. As most of the crowd thinned out considerably, young Doc Shaver took Longarm to one side to murmur, "I don't understand what's going on here. Do you suspect this dead breed was acting on secret orders from the powers that be in Sioux Siding?"

Longarm said, "He wasn't. That's about the only thing I'm sure of. No assassin acting under orders from the biggest froggy in this puddle would have had to bop the town lamp lighter on the head to black out that stretch of Market Street. Peg Leg Ferris would have done as he was told. Poor Pop Walters, dead inside, could have been taken to one side for a talking to by the boys in the back room. I'm still working on who ran Bram Drew out of town, or worse. See you in the back room in the morning,

172

Doc. I got to send me a mess of wires right now."

They shook on that and parted friendly, with the doc and a handful of local volunteers left to tidy up the death scene as Longarm and Gruff got on down to the all-night Western Union to send a mess or wires at full day rates so they'd arrive before bedtime, it being no later than nine P.M. as yet in spite of all the noise.

Having spread the word far and wide by wire, Longarm made his way back to Katrinka's by the back way, with Gruff backing his play in the dark with her keener senses, Lord love her. He told her she could have any and all innards Katrinka had saved from his own chicken.

Entering by the back gate, Longarm found the back-door locked but saved Katrinka coming down and climbing back up the stairs by unlocking the easy-going latch with the skeleton-key blade of his pocketknife.

As he and Gruff climbed the stairs, they saw the kitchen lamps were out. Longarm sighed and told Gruff, "She said they'd start without us if we didn't get back at a reasonable hour."

He struck a match to light the kitchen lamp and when he opened the icebox he found a whole bowl of chicken gizzards, livers and hearts. So he put them in Gruff's bowl near her corner pile of burlap bedding and called out he was fixing something for himself. He wasn't sure but he thought he might be hearing distant muffled laughter as he built himself some ham and cheese on rye. He washed the snack down with buttermilk and ambled on back through the railroad flat, calling out, "What's going on? Where the blazes has everybody gone?"

Katrinka's voice trilled from the front bedroom, "In here!" while she and her smaller brunette guest were laughing like hell, and dirty.

So he strode into the dimly lit front to join them, and there was just enough lamplight from the street out front to make out the position they were in, buck naked, as Katrinka sighed and said, "I warned you we might start without you. But now that I've seen what two girls can manage after all, I forgive you! Where have you been all this time?"

Longarm started to tell her as he hung his hat and gun belt handy, but then Katrinka was moaning, "Oh, yesss! Do it some more, Maureen! I'm going to come again, you naughty little thing!"

So Longarm took his time getting undressed and didn't join them, as bare of ass, before Katrinka rolled over on her broader beam to sigh. "That was lovely! I know what you're thinking, Custis, but you took so long and we got so hot after I'd been singing your praises upstairs and down."

From where the smaller gal's head currently reposed, with her jet-black hair unbound across the inside of Katrinka's pale thigh, Maureen declared in a sheepish tone. "I guess it was my fault. I hadn't had any for ages and when she reminded me how swell it felt I recalled how the other girls and I used to calm our nerves in this finishing school where I learned so much."

Longarm allowed he'd heard about such girls' schools and wistfully added he'd never gotten to go to one as somebody's soft she-male hand grabbed on to his manhood. He knew it was Maureen when she gasped, "Oh, my lands, you were right, Katrinka, he's manly indeed, and do you think he's man enough for the two of us?"

The bigger buxom blonde hugged the upper parts of Longarm to her heroic breasts as she declared there was only one way to find out. So Maureen steered his throbbing erection into her new pal as she declared, "Oh, I've always wanted to watch and from down here it looks so naughty but nice!"

Then, before Katrinka could come with Longarm the

petite brunette was up on her naked knees, pounding Longarm's bare back with her fists while she called out, "My turn! My turn! Hurry up in her and shove all that in me!"

Katrinka moaned. "Don't you dare take it out, Custis! I'll kill you both if you take it out *now* and . . . Yes, yes, yessss!"

Then she laughed, dirty, and said, "Go ahead and teach the greedy child some manners, Custis. Make her beg for mercy!"

So Longarm tried. But when he threw the blocks to the totally new experience of Maureen Flannery, rising to new heights in such new surroundings, the warm-natured Texican lived up to her spitfire reputation by taking him to the roots and reaching up for more with her trim horsewoman's pelvis to get more out of him than he'd thought he had to give her, fresh from the delights of the way bigger blonde.

After that, having discovered the delights of forbidden fruit, the two new chums wanted to get down and dirty, so Longarm let them, consoling his own conscious with the simple fact *he* wasn't queering anybody as he shoved it dog-style to Katrinka while she ate Maureen and, after a short break, reversed the process so the bitty brunette could go doggy and lizzy gal at the same time.

In the end, being only human, Longarm had to lie back and watch the two of them go at it awhile, until they inspired him to join in some more.

He'd lost track of how many times he'd come, in whom, when they snuggled close to either side of him and Katrinka commenced to cry on his shoulder.

Maureen told Longarm, "I cried like that the first time an older girl got me to eat her pussy. Isn't it odd how ashamed we can feel about things that feel so grand while we're enjoying them?"

175

Longarm dryly remarked, "I reckon it's a matter of taste."

Katrinka laughed through her tears and said, "God will get you for that. But you promise not to ever tell anybody here in Sioux Siding, don't you?"

He said, "I never . . . kiss and tell. Don't 'spect to be here long enough to talk that much to anybody about anything. As I was about to tell you ladies before I was so rudely interrupted, I'm about done up this way. I'm waiting on some last few answers by wire, come morning. But I figure I've got most of the pieces in place, now."

Chapter 20

Big frogs in little puddles might feel safe in keeping banker's hours, but Longarm woke up at cock's crow and despite a night to remember got up, got tidied up and proceeded to get dressed in his officious duds of tobbaco tweed while the two gals lay slugabed, fast asleep, with Mona Lisa smiles on their contrasting but equally pretty faces.

He was glad they got along so well, seeing it was about time to get it on down the road no matter whether anybody answered all those wires or not. For what was good for the goose was sauce for the gander and unlike Cherokee and other lovesick loons, Longarm had long since resigned himself to the simple fact that men and women both deserved somebody truer than themselves for themselves.

As he gently but firmly shut the kitchen door on old Gruff he told her, "I know you'll likely miss me as much or more, old girl, but you got to stay here. I ain't ready to bring any she-male back to my furnished digs in Denver."

He let himself out by way of the backdoor and worked

his way toward Uncle Pete's track by alleyway, breaking cover only at the last to check in with Western Union.

He found a slew of answers and saw addressing wires to home addresses after sundown on a sabbath had been sort of slick. Old Billy Vail's wire didn't say whether he or old Henry had been poring through the wanted files in the federal building late on a Sunday night, but somebody sure had, and his chat with Reverend Zimmermann over to the Lutheran church had paid off handsome.

Having neither the time nor the lead in his pencil to eat breakfast up at Magnolia Epworth's, Longarm found a trackside beanery patronized mostly by the railroaders, and the colored folks who ran it were proud to rustle him up a hearty breakfast of sausage and flapjacks with sorghum syrup and a side order of chili con carne, washed down with seriously black coffee.

So a couple of trains had come and gone and Longarm's hearty breakfast was settled enough to have him considering more coffee by the time he was properly set up to attend that hearing before Judge Boswell in the back room of the Warbonnet Saloon. The place had still been closed after he'd been up and about for hours.

The hearing was pro forma as before, with young Doc Shaver allowed to depose that the late Cherokee Adare had died from having his throat torn open then leaving to open his own damn clinic for Pete's sake.

That left Longarm with Judge Boswell, Uncle Roy Sanderson, a Deputy Wimmer Longarm hadn't met before and, of course, old Jubel Stark, sitting in as a sort of friend of the court.

Judge Boswell smiled up at Longarm to say, "The court sees no call to make you go over last night's events again, Deputy Long. Everybody here in Sioux Siding agrees the cocksucker had it coming and now that you've found out who else was aiming Big Fifties at federal law-

178

men in these parts you'll want to be getting back to Denver, right?"

Longarm asked if anyone had seen fit to notify their county coroner as custom required.

Judge Boswell replied, "Matter of fact I mean to wire him later this morning. He's only getting to his office about now. Since I mean to tell him this latest death was neither mysterious nor under local jurisdiction I doubt he'll pester you and the federal government about it. But if he wants to he'll know where to get in touch with you. So you are free to go, Deputy Long."

"There's a westbound for Cheyenne stopping here before ten," Jubel Stark declared firmly but not unkindly.

Longarm smiled down at the older big shot and replied, "I'm not going to make that one, Mr. Kraft. With luck, I could be on my way tommorow noon, though."

Jubel Stark, as he was locally known, just stared up thunderghasted.

It was Uncle Roy who asked, "Ain't you awake this morning, old son? How come you called Mr. Stark . . . What was that you just called him?"

"Kraft. Means the same thing as Stark in High Dutch. Both Stark and Kraft can be High Dutch names. Both mean Strong instead of bare-ass in High Dutch."

"I don't know what he's talking about," said Jubel Stark with a sneer.

Longarm said, "Sure you do, Jubel Kraft. Ain't nobody from the malarial gulf coast with such a name wanted for the same offenses."

Turning to Uncle Roy he explained, "As a lawman you likely know how crooks changing their names tend to choose new ones from the same old country and often with a similar meaning, not thinking why?"

He waited until the older lawman nodded thoughtfully and went on, "Had a hunch about this bird having a record

179

for what he's been pulling up here in Wyoming. When I noticed his new name worked as a High Dutch label, I got the Reverend Zimmermann to suggest some other versions in both English and High Dutch. Then I asked my home office to see if any of the suggestions fit as to probable age, prison records showing chronic malarial ague and so on. This morning, bright and early, Marshal Vail wired we have one and only one Jubel Kraft in our file of wanted fliers."

"Wanted for what?" asked Uncle Roy with a thoughtful look at the man who'd been pulling his strings for some time.

Longarm said, "I figured you'd know. Blackmail and extortion still on the books down Texas way or he'd have had no call to change his name when he came up this way to get in on the ground floor with the small fortune he'd extorted from a proud but weak-willed rich widow."

He let that sink in and added, "Since he ain't wanted federal for shaking down dirty old ladies in Texas you'll want to make the arrest up this way, Uncle Roy. There's a five hundred dollar bounty on his blackmailing ass and, best of all, he won't be able to blackmail any of you old boys no more."

He wasn't sure just how Uncle Roy had signaled Deputy Wimmer, but the next thing he knew something hard and firm was pressed between his shoulder blades and Longarm doubted it was Wimmer's finger.

He sighed and said, "Dumb move, Uncle Roy. I just offered all of you but Mr. Kraft, here, an easy out. You figure you can get away with the back-shooting of yet another federal lawman within earshot of the tracks?"

Uncle Roy gulped and pleaded, "Mr. Stark?"

Jubel Kraft aka Stark purred, "I don't see why anybody has to be shot within earshot of the tracks, Constable. I'm

180

sure he'll be proud to dig his own grave for you out on the open range a piece."

The local lawman almost sobbed. "Do we have to go that far, sir?"

The man who got to decide quietly replied, "We do. You just heard the man say he's out to have me arrested and shipped back to Texas. Needless to say, if anything like that were to happen I'd have no choice but to tell the law, and the newspapers, everything I know about . . . everything."

He nodded at Judge Boswell and added, "Hamish, fetch your surrey with the side curtains. We're going for a little ride in the country."

Longarm quietly asked, "What if I won't get in without a fight?"

The professional extortionist said, "You'll get in. And once we're out on the prairie you'll dig your own grave with Wimmer, there, covering you. I guess I know a thing or two about human nature, Deputy Long, and it's human nature to want to stay alive as long as one possibly can, at any cost to one's own wishes."

Longarm said, "I reckon you're right. Did you make Bram Drew dig one or two holes for him and his gal?"

Kraft-Stark chuckled and said, "Never had to. He was offered tickets to California and told the climate out yonder might be better for his health, so they left. I'm not an unreasonable man. I only kill people when I have to."

As Judge Boswell rose from the table Longarm said, "Stop and *think*, your honor! I don't know what he found out about you in those medical case books he helped himself to when Doc Eldridge died, but it can hardly be more embarrassing than taking part in a cold-blooded murder!"

Judge Boswell hesitated. But when Kraft-Stark said, "Do as I say!" the piss-poor excuse for a J.P. murmured,

"Sorry," and moved over to open the backdoor to the alley.

But as he opened it a sawed-off shotgun was shoved in his face, and a trio of hard-eyed trail-dusty men boiled in to throw down on everybody with two of them pointing a six-gun in each fist.

Uncle Roy gasped. "Sheriff Cohan! What in thunder are you doing down here in Sioux Siding?"

The county law Longarm had wired earlier and met up with way out on the edge of things around eight said, "Came down to see if there was anything to what this long drink of federal water said. At his suggestion we've been listening just outside, all the time, and you are all under arrest!"

Jubel Kraft, Stark or whomsoever, might or might not have meant to make a break for it, but as he sprang up from the table Deputy Wimmer shot him in the chest with the Schofield he'd been holding on Longarm. So Sheriff Cohan blew Wimmer away with a twelve-gauge shotgun blast and as those on their feet stood mighty still in the clearing gun smoke Uncle Roy sighed and said, "I never asked him to do that, Sheriff."

Cohan's voice dripped with scorn as he replied, "Tell it to the judge, you cocksucker!"

Which hardly seemed fair to others of his kind who only wanted to bring joy into their own little world.

Longarm knew he should have asked for a search warrant but he didn't see how he could, with Judge Boswell on his way to the county seat in irons. So he just busted into the fine house the late Jubel Kraft-Stark had built for himself and none of the help tried to stop him as he found the stolen medical case books and helped himself to the same.

He had plenty of time to go through them by the time he turned in his officious reports down in Denver. He laid out all the facts on paper and thus felt puzzled, the next morning, when the crusty Marshal Vail called him back to his oak-paneled inner sanctum for a sit-down conversation about the same.

Seated across the acre of cluttered desk from the older, shorter and dumpier Billy Vail, Longarm lit a cheroot in self-defense as his boss stared up from the report through the fumes of his awful cigar to say, "Most of this hangs together, old son. But you failed to nail down the exact *motive* for all Kraft-Stark's skullduggery."

Longarm said, "I don't put down what I don't know for certain. The boys in the back room shut him up before he could tell us anything I wasn't able to dig out of them medical tomes. If you want an educated guess, a professional blackmailer wanted for extorting a small fortune in Texas took it up to Wyoming to get in on the ground floor of a jerk-water stop that'll surely be a township someday. He bought cheap and sold or rented dear. He'd have done all right under his new name as an honest if hardheaded landlord. But as we both know, leopards have a time changing their spots, and once a thief always a thief. So when he had the chance to help himself to a dead tenant's case history books he did so, read 'em, and of course, reverted to type."

Vail nodded his bullet head and said, "I got the part about him blackmailing his way into the sort of ad hoc clique that had commenced to run things. Did Doc Eldridge come right out and say their half-ass constable and the foreman of the Rocking H were fairies?"

Longarm explained, "Not in so many words. Seems there's this medical condition called *proctitis*, which results from taking it up the ass more than one really should. Judge Boswell wasn't like that. He was a natural man living in sin with a woman not his lawfully wedded wife. Doc Eldridge had thought she looked awfully young and noted a strong family resemblance between them. Then there was the member of the ad hoc council who'd been bitten indelicately, trying to screw a family pet that wasn't in heat, and a really dirty old man who'd hurt the six-year-old daughter of his housekeeper with his man-sized organ grinder. The doc had made him promise he'd cut that out. No way of telling whether he did or not."

Vail waved his expensive but rank cigar and cut in, "I got all that. Any doctor making house calls sees and hears things a born blackmailer could use, and we know that sickly Texas blackmailer held what he had on them over everybody. But why did he try to obstruct you if he had nothing to do with the death of Pitcairn?"

Longarm shrugged and said, "He liked things the way they were, with the growing settlement unincorporated so he and his puppets could run things without political rivalry in an election year. As I said to poor Uncle Roy, and he agreed while the sheriff was cuffing him, they'd have been better off helping me instead of hindering me. I'd have never worried about anything that wasn't federal if they'd just let me do my job."

Billy Vail cocked a brow at him and observed, "But they didn't and in the end you wound up doing Sheriff Cohan's job for him. I notice Sheriff Cohan made those arrests a good three days and nights before you saw fit to head on home, Custis."

Longarm innocently replied, "Well, as I put in that officious report you just read, I had to stick around and tidy up some loose ends. Had to wire Sacramento and find out if Bram Drew was really alive. Then I had to go over the way Waco Walsh had diverted all that beef money with poor Miss Maureen's lawyer from Cheyenne and—"

"I'm sure Maureen Flannery was grateful," Vail cut in, adding, "Might this lawyer from Cheyenne have been of the she-male persuasion as well?"

Longarm blew a thoughtful smoke ring and calmly replied, "As a matter of fact she was. How did you figure that, boss?"

"Lucky guess," replied Billy Vail with a dry dirty smile.

Watch for

**LONGARM AND THE
COMSTOCK LODE KILLERS**

314th novel in the exciting LONGARM
series from Jove

Coming in January!

**Explore the exciting Old West with one
of the men who made it wild!**